Dear Monty
Dear Deborah

ISBN 9798848323580

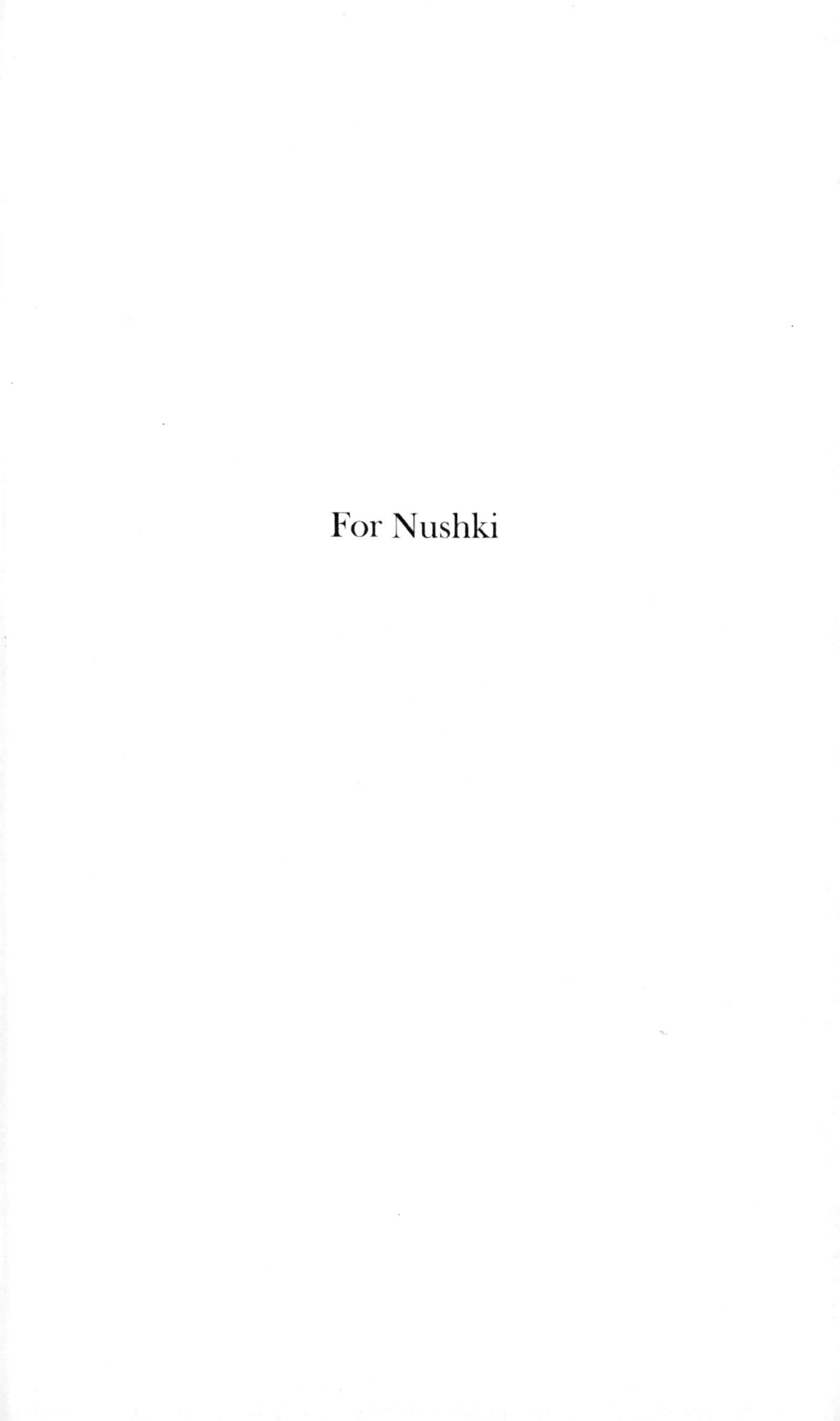

For Nushki

Tel Aviv
15th August 2006

Dear Mr S...........

I understand from your publisher that you have been researching Brigadier Montgomery Sutherland for a book. I have a considerable amount of material which might be of help to you in this matter, if you would like to contact me at the above address.

Yours

Yael Elon (nee Kapuchinski)

This letter changed everything, I cannot say I knew it at the time. It raised questions certainly. Who was Yael Elon, and why was it important to her to tell me her maiden name was Kapuchinski? Neither meant anything to me and, although my research covered reams of paper, I was pretty sure, without looking, that neither name featured in it.

And how had this woman got hold of my address, or come to that known about the book? All of this was a mystery and, having spent a year in one mystery I had no great appetite for another. To be honest, I let it go. I didn't even have the grace to reply and say not today thank you. I am ashamed of it now and, more importantly, ashamed as a researcher and writer that I didn't sniff out the bigger story at the time.

If it hadn't been for Yael's persistence, I should never have discovered the extraordinary correspondence between Monty Sutherland and Deborah Kapuchinski, her mother. Those letters revealed more to me about the man than the months of research ever had. I mean about the man himself, the man who loved Deborah Kapuchinski for thirty years - through all the history he made, moving among presidents and warlords, travelling the globe, sometimes publicly and sometimes clandestinely, but always loving one woman, wherever he was, thinking of her.

And just as it takes two to love, there turned out to be two people in this story, because Deborah herself has a history, a history that must be told with her lover's, if we are to understand, really understand.

Yael must have waited patiently for a reply from me, because it was more than a month later that I got another letter from her.

Tel Aviv
28th September 2006

Dear Mr S........

I have not had a reply to my letter so I hope you don't mind me writing again, as I cannot be sure it arrived.

I have in my possession almost a hundred letters from Brigadier Montgomery Sutherland to my mother, Deborah Kapuchinski, covering nearly thirty years. What is more, I believe that her letters to him may be at an address in England. Brig. Sutherland and my mother were lovers, and I believe their story will be important to your book about his life.

I hope I may hear from you soon.

Yours

Yael Elon

I sat with her letter in my hand, at my breakfast table, the french doors opening onto my Sussex garden. It had been raining a little and the late summer sunshine bathed everything in a gentle, watery light. It was peaceful, how I liked it. After my years as a reporter, living out of suitcases, staying in lonely hotels, I had come home to this, settled down to writing biographies, and enjoyed the peace I felt I had earned.

Now, though, my brain fizzed. All my old instincts came to the fore, and I smelled a story. I was right about that, but wrong about what the story was. This wasn't going to be the human side of a man who had shaped history, but I didn't know it then. It was only months later, when I finally read Brigadier Sutherland's letters in Worcestershire, that I realised the story was the letters. They told it better than I ever would be able to, and it was only then that I put it finally to the publishers that they should publish the letters themselves.

We got Yael's permission easily enough, and finally permission from his daughter for his letters to be published, and so, in the end, the only job I had was editing, piecing together the story, putting the letters in the right order, understanding what had happened between the two of them over all those years. In this task I was greatly helped when Brig. Sutherland's daughter found his memoirs, pages and pages of them, all hand-written, some neatly (obviously done at his leisure) and some scribbled hastily, I imagine between assignments, even on aeroplanes. She contacted me full of excitement about them, and when I arrived the next day at her home she had already gone through them herself, in her own need to understand her father better.

There are gaps, which is inevitable in a correspondence stretching over such a long time, and the reasons for these gaps will become apparent. I hope the reader will forgive me for attempting to fill in those gaps with my own understanding of what happened during that time.

I should set the scene for you because, unlike a biography, this story doesn't really have a beginning. The first letter is dated 1970, and is from Monty to Deborah. When I read it my mind was filled with what ifs. What if he hadn't written? Would Deborah have written to him instead? I didn't think so. What if she hadn't replied to his first letter? It occurred to me that could very easily have happened. After all, she had good reason to be angry with him and the whole story could have finished there. But something, I shall never know what, inspired her to reply, and so a great love affair was born. They, of course, didn't know that at the time.

Monty and Deborah came from such different worlds, and much of their lives they stayed worlds apart in what they did, but there were times when those worlds collided and the first, the biggest coincidence of all, is that they were both born in the same place in the same year. That year was 1946, shortly after the end of World War Two. They were children of the war in a way, as I suppose most people would say about themselves if they were born then, because who could come into the world at such a momentous time in the history of the world and not be a child of that time?

I said they were born in the same place. That was Cyprus, where Monty's father was commander of the military garrison. It was only four years since the German defeat at El Alamein and the garrison on Cyprus, like the other British possessions around the Mediterranean, breathed a sigh of relief at the rout of the German army in North Africa. The hero of the hour, General Bernard Law Montgomery, was much feted at the time, and by none more than Colonel John Sutherland on Cyprus. So much so that he insisted, it has to be said without his wife's complete consent, on calling his first-born son after their saviour.

A little later that year, Feigi Mandelstam gave birth to a baby girl in the detention camp for illegal Jewish immigrants to Palestine on Cyprus. She had been on her way from a displaced person's camp in Germany to start a new life in Palestine, and had boarded a ship at Marseilles, a ship barely seaworthy at all, let alone fit for the hundreds of refugees who crammed her decks. The British sailors who boarded the ship when it passed into Palestine territorial waters could hardly believe the mass of human misery they found. They took the ship in tow to Cyprus where holding camps had been set up, and there they imprisoned the Jews who had survived the Nazi concentration camps.

Feigi's husband had started the journey with her but somehow, somewhere, she had lost him. She couldn't remember where. The poor woman was no longer quite sane; she had seen too much and lost too much, and now no-one could quite make sense of her. When her baby was born it was taken straight to the camp nursery and when mother and child did finally arrive in the promised land they arrived separately, and in the chaos they were sent on separately to different camps for settlers. They were in fact eventually reunited, and by a bizarre stroke of good fortune, Feigi's husband one day simply turned up and claimed his family again. If Feigi was insensible before, this turned her completely and she never recovered her wits. Simon Mandelstam looked after his wife and brought up his daughter, learned Hebrew and worked the land of the moshav where the Jewish Agency settled them.

On Cyprus, running the camps was just one of the responsibilities Col. Sutherland had but not one he took a lot of interest in, leaving the day-to-day work to more junior officers. Mrs Sutherland and her baby son inhabited a world of comfort and privilege that was entirely unaware even of the existence of fifty thousand refugees on the island. Many years later, neither Deborah nor Monty had any memories at all of Cyprus, and found it hard to imagine they had both been there, albeit under utterly different circumstances, at the same time.

It was more than two decades later, and on another continent, that they met for the first time. Monty had himself gone into the army (it was expected he would) and by now was a newly-promoted captain of twenty-six, serving in Africa in a peacekeeping force that was trying to stem the bloodletting seemingly inevitable after hundreds of years of colonial rule. Deborah Mandelstam was a junior doctor from the Hadassah Hospital in Jerusalem, part of a group of volunteers for an Israeli medical mission in East Africa.

It will seem ironic that it was at a refugee camp that they met for the first time, at Olongwe. But this time it was Africans who were in the camp, and this time they were not prisoners (though Deborah felt they were, prisoners of their circumstances). Deborah and Issy Bar-On had met at medical school and were still together; in truth he followed her to Africa, it being rather more her idea to go than his. Issy was in love with Deborah; he was not sure she was in love with him, and neither was she, but they each accepted that fact for their own reasons.

Some of this fits in with my own researches and the rest it is possible to glean from their letters, particularly the early ones, but what I haven't been able to figure out is how Deborah became involved with Monty in the first place. Certainly Issy found out about the relationship, and he was definitely jealous, but when they returned to Israel they married, so I leave it to the reader to work it all out. All I can say is that love has no explanation.

So what sort of people were Monty Sutherland and Deborah Mandelstam? Looking at Monty's picture in uniform I would make the same assumptions as anyone who saw him in the newspapers during the nineties, as you probably did. He was the typical British army officer by his appearance. Smart, which almost goes without saying, with a strong face that gave him a very authoritative air. He even had a scar on his forehead coming down from the hairline to just above his left eyebrow. It was quite dashing and conjured up exploits of military daring that, whilst he had indeed had such exploits, did not apply in this case. The scar was nothing more than the result of a boyhood accident, an argument with some sharp object on falling out of a tree. And he was tall, and in my experience tall men get more respect than short ones, notwithstanding Napoleon and Hitler.

The uniform, of course, changes a man. Put a uniform on the mildest of men and he will see the world differently, and be seen differently. I know that from personal experience in the Territorial Army. The uniform made me a different person. But Monty had almost as much authority in civilian clothes. He dressed, it must be said, rather conventionally. In the picture he sent to Deborah, with his daughter Rosie in his arms, he is wearing a sports jacket with a check shirt and regimental tie. It's hard to imagine him dressed casually. Even in a picture of him with Deborah in Cyprus he is in white flannels and open-neck shirt, but still managing to look like a soldier. Perhaps that soldierly bearing is, then, what defines Monty Sutherland.

His letters, though, tell a different story. No-one writes letters thinking they are going to be read by strangers, particularly love letters, and I think I have to call them that. For that reason I don't feel entirely comfortable about publishing them, and I have asked myself why Rosie gave her permission. I think, like Yael, she sees them as a memorial to him. There is already one of those where he is buried, but the letters say more than a lump of stone can. Monty wasn't made of stone, and his letters aren't either, as you will see.

And what of Deborah? She is harder for me to

understand. Because she was a Jew, and an Israeli, I came to her with stereotypes in my mind, as hard as I tried not to. I hope Yael will forgive me for saying that her mother was not conventionally beautiful. Monty found her so but love, they say, is blind and I can confirm that from personal experience. Deborah had one of those faces that, as a man, I found at first fairly uninteresting but the more I look at her photographs the more I see in her. Naturally, I am influenced by her letters. By the time I had read them all I felt I already knew her and now, when I look at her face, I can hear her talking.

Of course it could be fancy, but I do imagine what her voice was like. She was an inveterate smoker, and Yael told me she had a smoker's voice, that sort of huskiness that in a woman can be quite sexy. She also spoke English with a slight American accent, having done some of her medical training in Houston. She was a quick-witted woman, and I can imagine she would have been a pleasure to talk with. I think also she was quite strong, the sort of person whom others would follow, but certainly the kind of woman that most men would follow.

I detect in some of Monty's letters a little jealousy, not just of her two husbands but of the men who undoubtedly desired her. I don't think Deborah's attitude to sex was ever casual, but I'm sure she did have lovers at various times. One thing I'm sure about though is that when she was married she was completely faithful.

What was the attraction between Monty and Deborah? What kept them coming back to each other over all those years? I don't know. For Monty, was it Deborah's foreignness, her slightly exotic looks? Did she have something of Carmen in her, a fatal attraction for men? That, perhaps, is a little fanciful, and yet when I look at her picture, look hard into her big dark eyes, I do fancy I can see how a man might drown there.

I think though it was more her personality that was the attraction, not just for Monty. Deborah laughed easily and that shows on her face. In all the photographs I have seen of her she is smiling, an easy, natural smile of someone who is comfortable with herself. Monty was, by all accounts, always a little insecure, and I suspect it was Deborah's sureness that kept him coming back. In his two marriages, and I don't know what other relationships he had, I don't think he ever found someone who gave him what Deborah did.

Olongwe
12th December 1970

Dear Deborah

I am giving this letter to Captain Stewart to post when he goes to the capital, in the hope that the postal system will work for long enough to get it on a ship for Haifa. As you wouldn't let me have your address, I am hoping too that the hospital will pass it on to you.

I know you are angry with me, even though you denied it when we parted. You can't see it, but I believe this is the only way. Issy loves you and you belong with him, in your own country, with your own people. What could I give you? I travel round the world, living in dreary bases when I'm back in England. The weather there you would hate. And the people, you know, army officers and their wives, not your sort at all. You would hate all of it.

And what about your own career? You know you have to pursue that in Israel, where you can do what you need to do.

We've had a wonderful time, and I'll never forget you. I want you to forget me though. You have so much to look forward to - don't look back.

With my very best wishes

Monty Sutherland

Jerusalem
January 3, 1971

Dear Monty

Your letter arrived at the hospital safely, but it was another week before anyone in the offices bothered to look me up.

I don't think you believe that I love you. If you did, you wouldn't say the things you did. Doesn't love matter more than those things? If we love each other, can't a way be found? I could retrain in England - my English is pretty good, you said so yourself.

Anyway, you don't want me, so I'll do what I'm told and be a good doctor and wife and live happily ever after in the promised land. You get on with your soldiering and get lots of medals and be a hero. I'll forget you before you forget me.

Yours

Deborah Mandelstam

Olongwe
14th February 1971

Dear Deborah

Just to prove you wrong, I am writing to show you, contrary to what you said in your letter, that I haven't forgotten you.

All the best for your future.

Monty

Jerusalem
March 8, 1971

Dear Monty

I haven't forgotten you either, now leave me alone with my unhappiness and get on with your wonderful life.

Yours

Deborah

Olongwe
29th March 1971

Dear Deborah

Look, I told you to go and be happy. I don't want to hear about unhappiness, so when you've stopped sulking write and tell me.

Yours

Monty

Jerusalem
April 22, 1971

Dear Monty

You told me to stop sulking. Frankly I find that a little insulting. What makes you think I'm sulking? I'm going away with Issy for a week, camping in the north, that's how much I'm sulking.

Yours

Deborah

Bulford Barracks
19th June 1971

Dear Deborah

I'm sorry it's taken me so long to reply. As you can see, I'm back in England. The company shipped back three weeks ago and the mail has only just followed us.

I really am sorry if I upset you. I thought it was a joke, but perhaps my English humour is too easily misunderstood. Do you accept my apology?

I do hope you enjoyed your holiday. I'm going on leave myself, to my parents' place in France. They won't be there, so I'll have the house to myself, which will be just what I need after Africa - peace and quiet, good food and wine, no responsibilities. I'm really looking forward to it. If I may, I'll write again when I get back.

With my best wishes

Monty

Jerusalem
July 12, 1971

Dear Monty

I'm sorry if you thought I was upset about your letter. You English - no sense of humour!

Was your holiday good? I trust you didn't overdo the food and the wine. But weren't you a bit lonely going on your own?

I am back at work now and the hospital is particularly busy. We are taking casualties from the IDF because the army hospitals are overstretched, so there's not much time for a social life. As you may read in your papers, things are pretty bad here. Not like Africa though, that was different, because we were stuck in the middle of the fighting, weren't we? Here, there is us and them, and that feels quite frightening.

Please write again soon.

Yours

Deborah

Bulford Barracks
7th August 1971

Dear Deborah

I read your letter with interest. I have been following events there in the papers. Do take care, won't you?

I had a wonderful holiday. I wasn't on my own all the time. The Rainsfords came out - they've got a house in the same village. We spent quite a lot of time together. Their daughter, Chloe, is an old, well, friend really. Nothing for you to worry about though, she's not much to look at, not like you.

Regards

Monty

Jerusalem
August 17, 1971

Dear Monty

I'm very glad you had such a good holiday. I don't understand why you think I would worry about you meeting up with an old girlfriend - I assume that's what this Chloe is, isn't she? You can do what you like. You have no responsibility to me.

Anyway, Issy and I are engaged now. So I don't think we should write to each other any more.

I do wish the very best for you and your future with Chloe or whoever you choose, and your career in the army. Issy is going back into the army here on secondment from the hospital for a year, they are so short of doctors.

So, best wishes again, and thank you for all you have given me.

Love

Deborah

Bulford Barracks
29th August 1971

Dear Deborah

Congratulations! Mazal tov - that's what you say, isn't it? So you and Issy are finally going to be married. I couldn't be more pleased. He's a good man (you're a good woman, too). I'm sure he will look after you and make you happy, and that's what I want for you - to be happy.

Chloe and I are thinking about that too. She wants to get engaged but I'm not at all sure. There's no hurry, is there? I mean I'm only 26. She's a lovely girl, and I'd be a fool to pass her up, but well, perhaps that's what I am. A fool, I mean.

Anyway, enough about me. I couldn't be more pleased (I said that already, didn't I?), so you give that man of yours my warmest congratulations and I look forward to an invitation to the wedding.

With my best wishes

Your friend

Monty

Jerusalem
September 17, 1971

Dear Monty

Thank you for your letter. You're thinking of getting engaged? I thought this Chloe was just an old girlfriend. When did all this happen?

Very best wishes

Deborah

Wessex House
Malvern
Worcestershire
12th October 1971

Dear Deborah

I'm spending a spot of leave with Chloe's parents before I go off to take up a teaching post at Sandhurst. I'll be there for some time. Brigadier Rainsford (Chloe's father) put me up for it. It will be a great boost to my career and I'm sure it's the best thing.

Actually, Chloe and I go back quite a long way, and I think her parents always thought she and I would one day get together. And we are, so everyone's happy.

Chloe knows I've been writing to you and made me kind of promise that I'll stop now, so this is my last letter to you. Well, all the best and so on. I won't forget you.

Monty

Royal Military Academy
Sandhurst
21st October 1971

Dear Deborah

I know I said I shouldn't be writing again, but I just read in the paper today about the action in the Golan Heights and I wondered about Issy. Just let me know he's OK, would you? You can write to me at the address above.

Regards

Monty

Jerusalem
November 8, 1971

Dear Monty

Thank you for writing and asking about Issy. I'm afraid I have some bad news. His field hospital was posted to the Golan in support of the army units there and on his second day there he went out to recover some wounded men. He was helping an injured man when he was hit in the back by a sniper. The bullet went straight through his spinal column and out again. He was almost uninjured apart from that, but the bullet has paralysed him below the waist. He was in the military hospital at first but I made a special request to have him moved to my hospital, Hadassah, so I could see him every day while I am working.

I visit him two or three times a day, depending on my workload. He's very depressed - as a doctor I can't pretend he's got a good chance of walking again, because he knows better. He has even offered to break off our engagement, but I have refused. For now, I can only pray.

I am sorry to write with such bad news, but it's the truth and I wanted to tell you. I promise to write with any more news.

Yours

Deborah

P.S. The man he was trying to save was a Syrian soldier, not one of ours. That hurts even more.

RMA Sandhurst
22nd November 1971

My Dear Deborah

I just had to write to tell you how terribly sorry I was to hear about Issy. I don't know what to say. How are you coping? In the years I've been in the army I've never been shot at, or even seen anyone shot at, so although we train for that sort of thing I can't imagine it. I suppose it's the difference between our countries - we train for war, but you live with it.

I insist you write regularly and keep me updated with his progress and I too will pray that he does make progress. He's a good man, and he didn't deserve this.

My thoughts are with you. I have told Chloe that I'm writing but that it's because of Issy and she says she understands, so it's all right for me to continue.

Love

Monty

There followed a long gap in their correspondence. In May 1972 Japanese terrorists massacred 25 people at Lod Airport near Tel Aviv (it's now Ben Gurion Airport). The murder was committed on behalf of Palestinian Arabs. These were difficult times in Israel and Monty naturally followed the events in the newspapers. He assumed, wrongly, that it was the reason for Deborah's failure to write.

Jerusalem
October 11, 1972

Dear Monty

It is a long time since I last wrote to you, nearly a year I think. Much has happened in that time and only now do I feel I can sit down and tell you about it.

Issy didn't recover from his paralysis. He begged me to end our engagement but I kept refusing. My parents agreed with him, and even his parents did, but I proved them all wrong and married him in the hospital. He was by then in a wheelchair and seemed to be making progress psychologically, coming to terms with his future - our future - under changed circumstances. The hospital had offered him a lecturing post, which I thought was wonderful, but the more good things happened the more depressed he seemed to become.

He came home to my apartment in Jerusalem - it's on the ground floor and I had a ramp made for him to get over the front step in his wheelchair. At last, after all the months, I thought he could see a future. His old friends from the hospital came to see him, and Uri Ben-Dovid, a friend from the army - he's a captain in the tanks. Uri must have given him his pistol. We found him on the roof - God knows how he got there.

After the shiva (the period of mourning) I went straight back to work. I thought it was for the best, but I couldn't concentrate. The hospital gave me some extended leave and I have been at my parents' apartment here in Jerusalem since then.

Family and friends have been very supportive, as you would expect. Many people here know what it is like to lose a husband or a son, or even a daughter, in this constant war but they get on with life again. I don't seem to be able to do that.

I'm sorry, I'm going to finish my letter here. I'll write again.

Yours

Deborah Bar-On

Monty didn't reply to this last letter from Deborah. By this time he had left Sandhurst and was posted immediately to 1st Battalion, The Royal Welch Fusiliers as Intelligence Officer. No sooner had he arrived there than the battalion went into training for posting to Grenada to deal with a military coup there. Deborah's letter must have languished somewhere in the military postal system, because it was much later, when the crisis had been dealt with and he returned to England, that Monty eventually received it. He was due some leave and rather than write he made the rash decision to fly to Israel.

I cannot say what was in his mind when he made this trip. Was it to be with Deborah to support her in her time of need? It didn't really look like that because time had passed and it was perhaps a little late to be consoling her. And in any case, some might say that a brief love affair two years earlier didn't put Monty in a position to be consoling the grieving widow, not to mention the fact that at the time of the affair Deborah had been with Issy anyway.

It's easy to make judgments about people's morals and say, 'I wouldn't have done that or, 'What kind of behaviour is that?' I have some admiration for Monty Sutherland, although I never met him, and perhaps I'm being more defensive of him that I should. All my training taught me to be dispassionate and not take sides, but this was no ordinary story. I did feel involved. After all, I met Yael, Deborah's daughter, more than once, and Monty's daughter as well. This wasn't just a story - these were real people, and, perhaps for the first time in my career, I was seeing the people behind the story.

Monty had married Chloe. I think they were happy enough, but reading between the lines I do detect some doubts in his mind. I think it was one of those marriages that worked without actually being a success, if you know what I mean. Whether he told his wife the reason for his trip to Israel, I don't know. Did he make up a story? If he did, that looks to me like deception, not something that's attractive in a young married man, but we can't assume he did deceive Chloe. Perhaps he even told her the truth. Was he strong enough to say, 'Look here, she's an old friend whose husband has died and I'm going to see what help I can offer'? He might have said that, and if he did how did Chloe respond? Did she know anything about his fling with Deborah? If she did, it's hard to imagine her letting him go to her, so one can only assume she didn't.

Monty had by now been promoted to Major, and I get the impression that he was starting to find his feet in the assertiveness stakes. He had had a minor command in the Antigua thing and was becoming a more commanding personality. Chloe was an army daughter and was well trained to become an army wife, so she knew something about accepting what was given to her.

I have been able to piece together some of what happened in Israel. Deborah was by then back in Jerusalem, working at the hospital again. Clearly, from his letters at least, some of the old flame was sparked (was it ever extinguished?) and equally clearly Deborah did not respond. Some of that was due to her loss, but Deborah went up in my estimation because Monty was now a married man and she had no intention of coming between him and his new wife.

I think, once they had established what their relationship could and couldn't be, they spent a few days getting to know each other again and I would date their real friendship from that time. When Monty returned to England he would have been able to look Chloe in the eye and tell her the truth - that he and Deborah were friends and she had nothing to worry about. A lot of wives would have worried anyway, but I have no way of knowing what Chloe really felt. Whatever it was, she seems to have kept it to herself. For then, anyway.

Monty's promise not to write to Deborah seems to have gone by the board, and he continued to do so. Did Chloe know? If she did, she said nothing, because I don't get the impression from his letters that there was anything clandestine about them.

1 RWF
Aldershot
20th March 1973

Dear Deborah

This is my new address. You can write to me at Battalion HQ.

I cannot tell you how good it was to see you again. I'm only sorry it was under such tragic circumstances, but I'm pleased to see how you are getting on now. If you don't mind me saying though, I think you are working too hard. Your new position at the hospital is wonderful, but isn't it time you learned to delegate? You can't take on the responsibility for every patient, you know.

Still, who am I to talk? My rank comes with a lot of responsibility too, but I've got Sergeant Major Baker and two very competent junior officers, and I'm learning to give them more work. Having the confidence to do that takes time to develop, I suppose.

Thank you for not sending me away. I wasn't sure how you would react, seeing me again so unexpectedly, but I am truly glad I came. Your country is wonderful. I don't pretend I understand it all. Why do you have to keep fighting? Why was Issy killed trying to save the life of an enemy soldier? When you said you have to be Jewish to understand these things I laughed, but back here, in the safety of England, I think I can see what you mean. I know you said I would never be able to understand, but give me credit for trying.

Going to Grenada helped because it was the first time I had been near any action. And although I was never actually in combat as such, I think it made it easier to imagine what it must be like living as you do, in a never-ending war.

And don't worry about Chloe. She understands, and hasn't said much since I got back, about the trip I mean - not that she doesn't talk to me! Anyway, I've got some good news. She's pregnant, so I'm going to be a father. I'm not sure how I feel about that yet - you're the first person I've told. One difference is that she's going to want a more settled life (she's already said that), so she may not always be able to accompany me on short-term postings.

In any case, the powers that be seem to have dumped me here for now. It's OK, but after Grenada I keep thinking I would like a more active posting.

Sorry - I've been rambling on, haven't I? I just want to add that you are in my thoughts. Maybe you shouldn't be, I don't know, but I don't think it can be wrong to have someone in your thoughts, can it? Even for a married man and father-to-be. Anyhow, that's how it is.

Keep well.

Yours

Monty

Jerusalem
May 1, 1973

Dear Monty

I haven't written for a while and you might have thought I wasn't going to. Well, I wasn't sure I was going to. I needed to think about what you said in your last letter - whether it's OK for a married man to be thinking about me. And whether it's OK for me to be thinking about you.

I confess that my first feeling when I read your letter was jealousy - of Chloe, I mean. She's got a husband and she's going to have a child. I have neither of those things. And I thought then it was time to stop this - whatever 'this' is. When you were here, at first I was unsure but then I decided it was alright. We're 'just good friends' as they say, aren't we? There's no harm in that, and I didn't feel we were doing anything wrong.

Now, with the news of your child, I'm not sure. Oh Monty, I'm sorry but I'm feeling confused. I think I'm supposed to say to you, stop writing to me, but if I do that I'll lose you, and if I'm really truthful I don't want to lose you. I can't explain why that is, because I don't understand it myself, but I just feel that way. I loved Issy, that's the truth, but in Africa I loved you too. Is that possible - to love two people at the same time? Perhaps there's more than one kind of love. I gave Issy my loyalty and I was a good wife, for the short time we had, but as hard as I try I cannot feel guilty for my feelings for you.

1 RWF
Aldershot
24th July 1973

Dear Deborah

You're quite right - we are just friends, and I promise that's all I want.

Thank you for your advice about not rushing off again. Actually, it's not my decision. I'm a soldier and I take orders. Sometimes they come from my regiment and sometimes from the Ministry of Defence directly, which overrides the regiment, but either way I just do what I'm told, go wherever and if I get killed while I'm there - well, that's what I signed up for.

I'm sorry, I shouldn't really have said that. I suppose I'm a bit off my job at the moment. Sometimes I think I really would prefer to be doing some real soldiering instead of this dull routine stuff. Half my time I'm at my desk and the other half is spent on petty matters like discipline, inspections and so on. It's a wonder the men don't go out of their minds. Their lives must be more boring than mine. Training only seems to have a point to them if they know they are being posted, but this endless training for its own sake they don't find stimulating and then discipline starts to suffer. They've got sport, of course, and that's a never-ending obsession with some of them, but there are always those who react badly to the boredom and get themselves into trouble.

It's funny isn't it - when you're on a posting all

you think about is getting home and when you're at home all you think about is getting away. Well, I got that off my chest, didn't I?

As it happens, life at home has taken a turn for the better. Chloe seems to be enjoying pregnancy and she also seems to be enjoying having me here. I think, as much as she was conditioned to army life long before I ever met her, she prefers the stability we have now. Dare I say it, the very ordinariness of life which bores me seems to suit her.

Her being in a better mood with me helps of course. I just worry that the thing that makes her happy is the thing that makes me unhappy. In the end, where does that lead?

I'm sorry to go on like this. You and Issy never had the chance to get bored, did you? I can't imagine life in Israel ever being boring. Perhaps a lot of people there wish it was. It's funny isn't it - everyone wants what they haven't got. It makes you wonder if what you haven't got is really any better at all.

On that philosophical note, I'll say good-bye.

Best wishes

Monty

Jerusalem
September 3, 1973

Dear Monty

I haven't written for a while - it's not deliberate, just pressure of work. Some of our doctors are on army service and one was seriously wounded, Mottie Silver. He was a friend of Issy's - they trained together. We've even been out a couple of times, nothing more than that, but I was very upset. He has lost the use of one arm, so his days as a surgeon are over. It feels a bit like Issy all over again, but I think he'll come through. His family are farmers up in Galilee and I think he'll go back there. A one-armed farmer is more use than a one-armed surgeon, and he's so strong, physically I mean as well, I'm sure he will make a go of it. And he can still fire a rifle, and up there men who can do that are going to be needed, I'm sure. So Mottie will go from saving lives, like me, to taking them, like you.

I'm sorry, I didn't mean to criticise what you do. After all, we are a country at war, so even as a doctor I completely understand the mentality of a soldier. Anyway, you haven't killed anyone for a long time have you? Actually, I never asked you - have you ever killed anyone?

I hope Chloe's pregnancy is going well. I am pleased to hear you two are getting on better.

Yours

Deborah

1 RWF
Aldershot
28th September 1973

Dear Deborah

Just a quick note to say how sorry I am to hear about your friend. I do hope it works out for him.

Chloe is absolutely blooming and happier than I have seen her since we got married. I'm taking some leave and we'll go up to her parents for a week or so before she has to get down to the serious business of giving birth.

Keep well.

Monty

Deborah didn't reply to this last letter. On 6th October, Yom Kippur, the combined Arab armies launched all-out war on Israel. The Egyptians crossed the Suez Canal before the Israelis knew what was happening. The Syrians attacked through the Golan Heights. For the second time since it was established by the United Nations in 1948, the existence of the State of Israel was in doubt.

Deborah's hospital was under extreme pressure and she slept in the shelter there when she was off-duty (which was never more than a couple of hours at a time). The staff listened to the radio constantly for news, not least for news of their sons and daughters, brothers and sisters, on the front line. Much of the time they didn't know where the front line was, and they knew that all their lives hung by a thread.

That thread held, miraculously. Given just a few days to gather themselves, the generals started the counter -offensive, and this time there was no doubt about who was going to be victorious. The Arab armies fell back, losing more ground than they had taken, and it was only by the intervention of the UN that the Israeli forces were prevented from driving into vast areas of Arab land.

Israel lived, but there were many wounds to lick, and for Deborah that meant constant streams of wounded - soldiers, civilians, adults and children. Her war wasn't over yet, until the last of the wounded were either sent home or buried. Finally, after weeks of gruelling work, she collapsed into a deep sleep for three days. At no time had she thought of Monty - he was part of another world which didn't concern her. It was only when she finally awoke to find the sun shining on her country one late October morning that her thoughts turned to him once again.

Most of this is of course in the public record, but the details of Deborah's life at this time were many years later related to me by her daughter Yael.

1 RWF
Aldershot
12th October 1973

My Dear Deborah

I am writing this in the hope that it arrives and finds you safe and well. I know it may take a while to get through to you. Naturally, I have been following the news every day (every hour actually) and have been able only to look on in horror, powerless to help, other than to pray (not a thing I do very often).

When you do finally get this you will know at least that I have been thinking of you.

Love

Monty

1 RWF
Aldershot
25th October 1973

My Dear Deborah

I am writing again in the hope that you receive this. I just had to tell you how I feel on hearing the news today about the ceasefire. As a professional soldier I am simply astounded by the way the IDF has fought back against such huge odds. The generals at HQ might have got it wrong, and undoubtedly Israeli Intelligence was way off the mark, but your people are brilliant. I have never seen an army fight like that. As you can tell, I am lost in admiration (and not a little jealous).

Nevertheless, my happiness will be constrained until I know you and your family are all right. Please write as soon as you can, or even better telephone, and let me know. You can call the regimental office and leave a message for me.

Love

Monty

Shortly after this letter Monty was posted to Northern Ireland in an Intelligence role, and he was incommunicado for nearly a year. Before he left, he made a rare telephone call to Jerusalem to inform Deborah (from his office at the Ministry), so she wouldn't worry about not getting any letters from him for a while.

Unsurprisingly, she worried all the more. She had only a vague idea about what was happening in Ulster, but her experience of living in a country at war (let alone of course the death of her husband in that war) told her that it was likely to be dangerous. Monty couldn't tell her why he was going, which was just as well. Even Chloe didn't know that.

Chloe had her baby shortly after he left, a girl, whom she named Rosie after her grandmother. When Monty returned he was overwhelmed with love for his daughter, who was already over ten months old. After a while they started to feel there was something wrong with her and tests showed that Rosie was deaf. Monty just loved her all the more for her disability, but Chloe seemed to be rejecting her, which distressed him of course.

Monty made a number of trips back to Northern Ireland. Naturally, there's not much known about these assignments, but on each occasion an undercover guard was put on his married quarters on the base. Chloe didn't know about this of course - it would have worried her more than she already was.

Wellington Barracks
London
20th November 1974

My Dear Deborah

I can write to you again, at last. I can't tell you about my work, but I can tell you I'm safe and well. As you will see from my address, I'm not at Aldershot just now. Chloe and the baby are there and they're fine. I didn't get a chance to tell you when I rang but, although Rosie is a healthy baby she is deaf. It's come as a blow, not least to Chloe - she seems to have taken it particularly badly. Rosie of course doesn't know she's deaf, bless her. She's such a happy child. You would love her, I'm sure.

What am I doing here in London? Well, I can't say too much, but it's a posting at the Ministry of Defence. I'm commuting each week (it's like being an office worker!) and I get back to the family at weekends. I'm putting up at these barracks while I'm here. It's comfortable enough - I dine in the officers' mess, but they're not sure what I'm doing here so it's a bit cold on the social front.

Things are a little cold with Chloe as well, so in a way I'm quite glad to get away, but I do miss the baby though. I miss you too.

Love

Monty

Wellington Barracks
London
15th February 1975

My Dear Deborah

I'm sorry I haven't been able to write for a few weeks. I've been abroad, I can't say where, and back to Northern Ireland briefly as well - just routine stuff, not in the danger zone, so there's nothing to worry about. I'm very glad to hear that you worry about me. I'm not sure Chloe does. In fact I'm not sure she misses me very much.

I have spoken with the army doctors about Rosie and they say there's nothing that can be done. She will always be deaf I'm afraid. Anyway, she's such a happy child it's hard to worry about her. I think she will always make her way in life despite her disability.

It was her first birthday recently, and I managed to get home for a couple of days. Things with Chloe weren't any better and in that way I was actually quite pleased to get back to London again. I've brought back a picture of Rosie, which I keep on my desk. I don't have a photograph of you, do I? Would you mind if I have one?

By the way, if you don't hear from me for a while, don't be surprised. I may have to go away again, but if I do I'll try to call to let you know.

Love

Monty

Jerusalem
March 16, 1975

Dear Monty

I did enjoy your last letter. I don't know why, but I like to get your news (even when it's not always good news). When I read your letters, I can hear your voice, your deep comforting voice.

It was Issy's yorzeit last week (that's the anniversary of his death). It was hard, and I'm afraid I got quite depressed, and it made me worry more about Avrom, but I'm better now. I spent a couple of days with Issy's parents, and that helped. We seem to have got closer again recently, which is strange, but perhaps it's because we need to share him now.

By the way, please send me a photograph of Rosie. I would like very much to see what your daughter looks like. I can't imagine what your life is like there, what your wife looks like, or your home. Because I have been to England, I know the sort of houses you live in, and what your streets and towns look like - different from here. I'm thinking about whether I should send you a picture. Would you be able to keep it somewhere safe? You know what I mean.

If you are going away please do telephone if you can to let me know. And take care.

Love

Deborah

Monty seems to have got this letter just before he left again for Northern Ireland, and didn't have time to respond to it. Whether he was able to call Deborah before he left I don't know, but I imagine so. He was gone for several months.

During this time an undercover guard was again put on his house in the Aldershot camp. It was this, paradoxically, that brought about the end of his marriage. It was the guard's duty to report all visitors to his house, and a sergeant in the Royal Military Police noticed that the same man was visiting Chloe, often late at night. When he started staying until the morning this put the sergeant in a difficult position, but he had to report it to his senior officer.

Chloe's visitor was an army officer and the MPs brought him in and faced him with the evidence. I suppose they had hoped he would be scared off but it seemed to have the opposite effect. When the Military Police captain went to see Chloe, she refused to end the relationship and, rather than have Monty informed by the army, she promised she would tell him herself. When Monty returned from his assignment, she told him she wanted a divorce.

He was devastated. He must have been under considerable stress after his assignment in Northern Ireland and he handled this revelation badly. He had a screaming match with Chloe in front of Rosie who, although she could not hear them could have had no doubt that her mother and father hated each other. Monty took her to his parents' house and they looked after their son and granddaughter while Monty calmed down.

He had to accept what was a fait accompli. He suddenly realised he didn't love Chloe, and it felt almost like she had released him from his commitment to her, the commitment he made when he promised, in the wedding service, to love her for ever. Suddenly, he felt elated and free.

What he also felt was concern about Rosie. Under the

circumstances, he was very reluctant to hand his child over to his unfaithful wife and a fellow army officer who had cuckolded him. In the event, Chloe didn't want Rosie, which in a way relieved him but at the same time made him terribly sad for his daughter's sake. This left him with a considerable problem though. Most men would find it difficult to bring up a child on their own, but in Monty's job it would have been impossible. It was his mother who came to the rescue. She doted on Rosie and had little difficulty persuading her husband that the little girl should live with them.

Who knows what's in the mind of a small child, let alone one who's deaf? All I do know is that the arrangement worked well. Rosie thrived; she gave her grandparents a new lease of life, and it even meant they saw more of their son, who inevitably became a regular visitor.

1 RWF
Aldershot
30th January 1976

Dear Deborah

Well, my latest news is that Chloe is divorcing me. That's not strictly true, because under English law she can't, because I haven't done anything wrong - she has. So I'm divorcing her, because she asked me to. She wants to marry again (the officer she had the affair with) and frankly I don't care what she does, so I'm going ahead with it.

Rosie has settled down amazingly well with her grandparents. When I go to see her I even feel sometimes that I'm intruding on their happy life together. It's probably not true, but I feel that way. I think I'm just feeling a bit lost at the moment, not sure what I'm supposed to be. Am I Rosie's father? I don't mean that literally (although it did occur to me) but does she need me now? I believe she does, but when I see her with my parents I'm less sure.

The Ministry won't send me back to Northern Ireland, because I have a dependent child. That leaves them at a loss to know what to do with me and for now they've dumped me back with my battalion, but they're not sure what to do with me either, because I've been away so much there's no role for me.

Ironically, Chloe's father has some influence with the Ministry (so does my own father, but he wouldn't use it) . Actually I'm not sure you would call it influence so much as just knowing the right people. He's offered to help. I think he is embarrassed about what's happened and wants to do something for me to make amends for what his daughter has done. That's my amateur psychological assessment anyway.

Either way, I'm here for now and we'll see if he lives up to his word.

I love the picture. You haven't changed - I don't think you ever will. You're still beautiful (I can say that now). Seeing your parents, looking so frail, I feel even more guilty for writing to them, but what's done is done. And your brother - you're right, nothing like a British soldier at all. Frankly, I can't imagine him hurting a fly, let alone killing a man, but he does have a kind of look, what we would call cocky. I've seen that in some of my own men - it comes from being part of a brotherhood, in which they give each other courage.

If you are allowed to, tell Avrom from me to take care. He doesn't have to prove anything.

Love

Monty

ever known in England. It was like his own parents' drawing room, or Chloe's parents'. This really was a bit of England in the Middle East. It made him feel at the same time comforted and uncannily disturbed, homesick despite the attempt that had been made to make him, and everyone else there, feel at home.

For the first time in his life he thought about what it meant to be British. He hadn't thought it in Africa, or on any of his other postings. He says in his memoirs it was Deborah who put this thought in his mind, because for the first time in his life he cared about someone who wasn't British, who didn't share that, and all it meant, with him. It occurred to him suddenly that he had never stopped to consider who he was, where he fitted in the world. He wasn't jingoistic, he simply had always taken his nationality for granted. You can never really know what that means though until it is tested, and he seems to have felt at this time that was what was happening.

It wasn't even about loyalty. He couldn't imagine being disloyal to his country, and yet at the same time he felt that being British wasn't enough, wasn't what life was for, if I understand what he says in his writings. There had always been other people, other nationalities, but now there was someone, someone foreign, who meant as much to him as anyone he had ever known. And that someone was in a country at war with the very one where this little bit of England sat. That put Deborah out of his reach, further away, much further, than she had been from Aldershot. He slumped on his bed and felt very sorry for himself.

As he surveyed the room, his dress uniform was hanging, freshly pressed for him, on the wardrobe door. He put it on and went to the ambassador's residence for the dinner being held in his honour.

In fact Monty seems to have settled well into both his new job and the life in Amman. He was given access to bases of the Arab Legion and was not unimpressed with their level of training and equipment. Since Britain was paying for it he was not surprised.

He was also given access to every unattached British female in the city. It was expected that he would accompany someone's daughter to social functions, and with his looks, not to mention the uniform, there was no shortage of claimants on his arm. He found this part of his duties not unpleasant, and yet he found too that he couldn't match the eagerness of these young ladies (let alone their parents, for whom potential sons-in-law were few and far between in Jordan). Some say absence makes the heart grow fonder and this applied to Monty. He received regular letters from Rosie, and spoke with his parents about her on the telephone occasionally, but he hadn't had a letter from Deborah in months. He kept a photograph of both of them on his desk ; this at first produced comments from the secretaries about his lovely little girl and how he must miss her (which was true) and from the men about Deborah, whom they took to be his girlfriend (which wasn't).

He confided in the First Secretary that Deborah was Israeli and was advised that he could not write to her, as the Jordanian postal service would not deliver mail to the Israeli postal service. Eventually it occurred to him that he could get a letter to her via England, and he wrote to a friend in his regiment to ask if he would act as a post box for them. All of this took time and it was another few weeks before he got his first letter back from Deborah. His first letter to her, unfortunately, is missing.

Jerusalem
April 19, 1977

Dear Monty

Yes please. Let's meet, somewhere, I don't know where. I wish I could talk to you on the telephone. It would be so much easier to make arrangements. Anyway, write and let me know what you think, how it could be arranged.

Love

Deborah

British Embassy
Amman
22nd May 1977

Dear Deborah

It's all arranged. I hope you can fit in with the dates (from about 14th July), so please let me know as soon as you can. I have to fly to England to report to London personally. That will only take a day, then I'll go down to Woking to see Rosie. My father still has a small house on Cyprus and I'm going to take Rosie there. You said you wanted to meet her, well, this is your chance.

Can you come to Cyprus? I've made enquiries, and you will have to fly to London first. Perhaps we can even meet up there and fly on together? Do write and tell me you can make it.

Love

Monty

her onward flight to Tel Aviv. He thought he might just arrive before she left, the hope being that he could present his parents with a situation, that was him, and Rosie and Deborah for their, their what? I think he wanted their approval.

It didn't turn out like that though. As he entered the Heathrow terminal building he was approached by two men who flashed warrant cards at him just long enough to show where they came from, and without a word they escorted him to a waiting car. No passport formalities are necessary, apparently, when H M Government wants to talk to you.

As Monty sat in an oak-panelled office in Whitehall, it was revealed to him what kind of trouble he was in. The man the other side of the desk wanted to know what he was doing in Cyprus with an Israeli citizen, one Deborah Bar-On, nee Mandelstam, a doctor at Hadassah Hospital in Jerusalem, and widow of an Israeli soldier killed in action. Monty's first reaction was to correct them about Issy being a soldier, but it was a bad move, because it just confirmed for the man behind the desk that Major Sutherland knew these people. Of course he knew them; he was Deborah's lover - and this man knew all about it.

What he didn't know, and would very much like to, was what else Monty had to do with the Israelis. Monty wasn't at all sure what was meant by 'the Israelis', as if he was in some way working for them. It was at that moment that the penny dropped. You would think that an Intelligence Officer of his experience would have figured it out already, but he was too close to see it. This was too ridiculous for him even to have thought of it. Normally he would have been one step ahead of his interrogator but at the moment he was at a disadvantage.

It was the one thing, as he racked his brain just a couple of days before on Cyprus, that didn't occur to him. That the people who were following them were from his own side.

What occurred to him now, as he fought the tiredness that was finally catching up with him, was that, on the assumption that MI6, or whoever he was talking to, didn't actually go bumping off British Army officers, he had lost a night's sleep for nothing. So silly did he think this whole thing was that it was literally all he could think of at that moment.

When he got beck to Aldershot the first thing he thought of was to speak with Deborah. But if the security services had gone as far as Cyprus to follow him, he didn't think they would have much problem tapping his phone, so he wrote instead.

1 RWF
Aldershot
1st August 1977

Dear Deborah

I am writing instead of phoning, because as hard as it seems to believe, I do not trust the telephone. The whole world seems to have gone mad, and maybe I have too, but I don't know who or what to trust just now.

I know now that you were met at Heathrow by someone who didn't introduce herself (but I can tell you she was from British Military Intelligence) and that she put you on a flight straight to Tel Aviv. I know they brought my father with them to collect Rosie, so at least she was taken care of. I don't know much more than that, as far as concerns what happened to you.

There was some suggestion, when I was questioned in London, that your own security people were going to be informed anonymously about you seeing a British Army Intelligence Officer posing as your 'boyfriend'.

I have been trying hard to think not only why they have got this so wrong but how. The only conclusion I can come to is the First Secretary at the embassy in Amman. I did confide in him about you, but I never thought he would come to such a ridiculous conclusion, let alone inform on me as a potential security risk.

When I landed at Heathrow I was taken straight to London and interrogated. I'm in all sorts of trouble. I'm not going back to Jordan - they are packing up my things and sending them over. I imagine they will go through them looking for, well I don't know what. I don't think they can really believe I was passing State secrets to you, because if they did surely they would have detained you at the airport. I think they are just jittery. Anyway, please write immediately and tell me what has happened at your end, whether there has been any trouble for you.

I'm really very sorry for this. It just didn't dawn on me on Cyprus that it could possibly be our own people. That night I spent sitting, watching over you and Rosie, thinking the IRA were after me. I must have an exaggerated belief in my own importance (mind you, it seems MI6 do as well).

Well, now I'm back here, confined to barracks pretty well. They've told me not to go anywhere while they continue the investigation into my case. I didn't even know I had a case. I'm afraid I have found the whole business so stupid I haven't been as co-operative as I should, and in the army that counts against you. If it weren't for my work in Ireland I think they would take this further, but there are people in high places (strangely, including Chloe's father) who don't want to lose me. So for the moment at least I'm worth more to them alive than dead (figuratively speaking) so I think they will leave it a while for this to settle and then look for some job for me where I can't do any damage.

It's probably the end of my career, at least as far as promotion is concerned. Where I go from here I don't know. Honourable discharge and a *job in the City, or work out my service riding a desk, as we say. Still, for the moment I don't have to make any decisions, because it's in their hands.*

Meanwhile, I'm shuffling papers and driving over to my parents' to stay with Rosie most nights. She seems to have forgotten the whole thing, but that's children I suppose. My father is very concerned about me. He wants to believe I'm not some kind of double agent, because I'm his son, but his military mind makes him suspicious, even of me. That bothers me more than the security services - they can think what they like. Anyway, he's advised me to break off all contact with you, which by the way I have no intention whatever of doing. I haven't done anything wrong and I don't see why I should apologise.

I'm attaching an address on a separate piece of paper that you can write to, as a mailbox. Any letters from Israel to me will automatically be opened, so you can't write here. Good grief, I'm starting to think like a spy.

Love

Monty

[Editor's note. That address has never been found, so I don't know who the mailbox was. Was it the same officer who provided this service for Monty when he was in Amman?]

1 RWF
Aldershot
25th September 1977

Dear Deborah

I wrote to you weeks ago but I haven't heard back from you. Please write and let me know whether you got my letter will you? Naturally, I am worried, so please do write.

Love

Monty

1 RWF
Aldershot
7th October 1977

Dear Mr Mandelstam

I have written to you in the past and I do hope you will not mind me writing again now. I have not heard from Deborah since she returned from Cyprus and whilst this might be difficult for you please try to understand my concern for her.

I can only ask that you ask Deborah to get in touch with me please.

Yours sincerely

Major Montgomery Sutherland

NETANYA
NOVEMBER 22,1977

DEAR MAJOR SUTHERLAND

PLEASE EXCUSE MY ENGLISH. DVORAH ASKS ME TWO WRITE SHE WILL WILL NOT WRITE AGAIN.

SORRY.

REUBEN MANDELSTAM

Monty's memoirs from this point are a bit of a jumble and not consistent with his normal ordered style. Clearly he was in turmoil. I could understand when I read them what must have been going through his mind. His own life was falling apart but he never stopped worrying about Deborah. He had no idea what was happening in Israel. Had she been told to stop writing or was it her own idea? Was she angry with him? All he knew was that she was well; otherwise, he felt, her father would have mentioned it. In desperation, whether they were tapping his phone or not, he telephoned the Hadassah Hospital but they said she was busy, and she didn't return his call.

His relationship with his father deteriorated now, as the older man thought his son was making a fool of himself. He no longer believed Monty had done anything wrong but he did think he was behaving badly and said so. I suspect Monty knew he was behaving badly, but who can say they would not in such circumstances? He even shouted at Rosie on one occasion, something he had never done. Rosie, apparently, could tell when she was being shouted at without needing to hear the sound of it.

To make matters worse Chloe got to hear about what had happened (I suppose through her father) and started phoning Monty over silly things to do with Rosie that she had never bothered about before. Monty was in no mood to mess with her and said so in no uncertain terms, which got back to her father and he thought that probably some spook somewhere in Whitehall was making notes of all this in his file. He started to feel no-one was on his side and I should say at that time he was right.

He comments more than once that he just wanted to get away on some posting. He volunteered to go to Northern Ireland, if not in an Intelligence role then in any role, but this was turned down and he went on exercises in Norway with his battalion. The climate there seems to have cleared his head somewhat and he returned after a month of hard work feeling refreshed and more purposeful.

He had hoped there would be a letter from Deborah on his return but there wasn't. For a while he dithered about writing again but it seems in the end he didn't. I can't say whether he should have. Would Deborah have relented with one more letter? He didn't even know if she could write, so he veered between being angry with her for her silence and worried about the same silence. Time, though, changes everything, and Monty got on with life. The months became years and without a war to fight he spent his time serving his country by not doing very much.

It was this not doing very much that in the end was to benefit his career, because the Ministry of Defence likes no man better than one who keeps his nose clean. Soldiers who get in the news (as long as its for the right reasons) are good for recruitment, but the soldier who just gets on with the job tends to rise faster. In due course Monty found himself with a clean slate and promotion, in his early forties, to Lieutenant-Colonel. He didn't know it, but someone was still pulling strings on his behalf.

Having given him another pip on his shoulder, the Army was sort of obliged to find him something more useful to do. He was still nominally attached to First Royal Welch Fusiliers, but yet again he received a posting quite separate from his batallion. It was at this time that he wrote again to Deborah. It was a strange thing to do, not just because it had been such a long time but because he never posted the letter. I found it bundled in with his memoirs and I knew immediately I wanted to include it. I did ask his daughter specifically about it and after reading it she agreed with me, because it says so much about her father.

gone ahead, for Rosie's sake, but she's old enough now that she doesn't need another mother.

I know I'm foolish for carrying a light for you all this time, but I am a fool and that's that. I know I'll never have you. Well, I tell myself that, but perhaps I'm not being completely truthful. Perhaps I say it because I daren't believe it's possible, to protect myself. Am I still in love with you? Well, with Chloe I can truthfully say I don't still love her. That love came to an end. But with you - it never came to an end. We didn't fall out (as far as I know, anyway). You have never told me it ended, and I have never wanted it to. So it's unfinished business, as we say. I'm not wasting away for the love of you, no, that would not be true to say. But on the other hand I can't forget you. So that leaves me in no-man's land.

Am I going to carry this weight for the rest of my life? Maybe I will. I realise this would sound terribly silly to anyone reading it, but since no-one is ever going to I don't care. It's taken me all this time to write it and I feel better already for doing so.

So I'll live. But wherever you are, whatever you're doing, I only hope that one day you will think of me and come and find me.

With my love

Monty

By one one those odd chances that life throws up when you least expect it, very soon after Monty wrote this letter he received a posting. It was this posting that changed his career but it also had an unexpected result that changed his life in other ways too. Apart from anything else, it lead directly to what happened in Chechnya, and that really did change his life. It nearly changed all our lives.

In an age when the British Army fought only sporadically, Monty's opportunities for action were few and far between, and he was destined to serve his country in a different capacity. His experience in Intelligence, both in Northern Ireland and, albeit briefly, in Jordan, combined with his very impressive natural skills, made him a commodity in short supply. It wasn't long before those skills were needed, this time as a NATO liaison officer with the United States military at the Pentagon in Washington.

An immediate promotion, to full Colonel, went with the posting and, from his memoirs, he seems to have relished the job, not to mention the rank, which equalled his father's now. His only regret was leaving Rosie again, but she was at a special boarding school and he had to accept that she didn't need him to be there. Their relationship was, by all accounts, an especially close one, despite not seeing each other a great deal, and Monty had no doubt that his daughter loved him as much as he loved her. Rosie has confirmed that to me herself.

What's more, I think they had a lot of mutual respect. Rosie, understandably, was proud of her father's rank in the army, and the important job he did. Monty, in turn, was proud of her. His notes show a sneaking admiration for his daughter, an understanding that, notwithstanding his own formidable intellect, she was going to outshine him. He would have loved her regardless, but there is definite pride in the way he describes her development, and hopes, notwithstanding her deafness, for a good career for her. He didn't know what a deaf person can achieve but he had a feeling she would break through the barriers it normally imposed.

So he took his leave of her and his father and in due course settled into his new office in Washington. He found everything in America fascinating. It wasn't his first visit, having spent two weeks with Chloe touring New England, with a brief visit to New York. It was the Spring when he arrived and, although he found the weather not dissimilar from the south of England, the air somehow was different, and he found that refreshing.

Every time I have visited the US I have been reminded what a very different place it is, and how different the people are. Whatever their racial origins - black, white, Asian, whatever - it seems to me they are first and foremost American and I can see what it was that Monty found in them that he liked. Dare I call it a simplicity, or perhaps lack of sophistication, that, to put a positive slant on it, I find honest, certainly when you come from Europe.

He enjoyed his new job and for the first time in years he became more social. It was hard to avoid invitations proffered in genuine hospitality. He was good looking, of not-inconsiderable rank and, for Washington hostesses especially, single. It was like he had gone back all those years to the days when army mothers in England sought his company for their daughters.

I think in fact he was a bit overwhelmed by some of those charming young American women and in no time he found it not too hard to be agreeable. In other words, at last there was something to bring him out of the place he had secluded himself in since Deborah. Nevertheless, he had no intention of getting too serious with anyone and, in any case, his work kept him pretty busy. As well as liaison duties at the Pentagon, he managed to wangle an invitation onto the occasional exercise, first in the deserts of New Mexico with the US Marine Corps and then a few months later, for a complete change, with a specialist unit doing ski training in Canada in conjunction with a company of the Royal Greenjackets from England.

These were diversions though, because he had serious work to do. Even in his memoirs he didn't divulge a lot of detail about what he was actually doing in Washington, and most of it is still governed by the Official Secrets Act. But because of the public enquiry after Moscow, some of this early material is now in the public domain.

It was in Washington that he met Avrom Mandelstam. Avrom, of course, would not have known him but Monty had seen Avrom's photograph and whether Monty had a good memory for faces, or Avrom resembled Deborah, I don't know, but as he walked down a corridor in the Pentagon he saw this face and something in his brain made a connection. He stopped in his tracks and the young man walked on, puzzled as to why a stranger was staring at him but otherwise untroubled. He didn't look back but Monty turned and watched the back of his head, trying to figure out why he knew him. The context was wrong, and all he could do was shake his head, as if by that action he might shake out the answer.

Avrom wasn't in uniform, but in a business suit, which put him yet further out of context and, as hard as Monty shook his head, no answer came. He sat through a meeting paying less than full attention to the business at hand. He was troubled. He told himself not to be silly - it was just someone who looked like someone, but it wouldn't go away. In the canteen at lunch he sat down and tried to busy himself with a day-old copy of the Times. As he sat there he heard a chair scrape on the floor and there, when he looked up, was Avrom.

The latter addressed him by his name which, until he remembered it was on a badge on his uniform, threw him yet again. And Monty, without knowing how he did it, suddenly knew who he was and called him Avrom. This threw the young man into considerable consternation but Monty stood up, told him he knew his sister, and offered his hand. After just a couple of seconds to compute all this information, Avrom did the inevitable and took his hand, upon which they sat down and talked.

Avrom was by now a captain in the Israel Defence Forces, but he didn't volunteer the name of his unit, and Monty was wise enough in these things not to ask. Since Israel was not a member of NATO there had to be some special mission that placed an IDF captain at the Pentagon. Monty was able to tell him freely (well, probably not all that freely) about his posting there, and then Avrom asked the obvious question - how did Monty know his sister?

It occurred to Monty then that Deborah had told no-one about Cyprus. Was it because she was too angry about what had happened, or because someone had told her not to? Their father could have told Avrom about Monty's letters, but apparently hadn't. So Monty decided to keep it simple, and told him about Africa. He had to add that they had corresponded, otherwise how would he have had a photograph of Avrom and how would he have recognised him? The explanation seemed to satisfy anyway.

Monty asked about Deborah and when he heard that she was married it was all he could do not to show the shock on his face. In fact Avrom was skilled at looking at someone without them thinking he was; he saw Monty's reaction and he knew immediately. Just as he could see what people were thinking, he could hide what he himself was thinking, and Monty saw nothing in his face. Of the two men, I have to say Avrom was very much better at the kind of work they both did. Monty was clearly a frank and open man, one who wasn't in fact hard to read. In most aspects of life, not least in relationships, that is an admirable quality.

In Intelligence work it can be a disadvantage.

Monty's memoirs at this point go into quite a lot of detail about Avrom. He took to the young man I think not just because he was Deborah's brother but because he was a very personable young man. What he didn't know was that Avrom was making himself personable for a reason, something he did quite easily and one of the reasons he had been selected and trained for this work.

Despite their age difference, Monty found he was socialising more and more with Avrom. He took him to some of the parties he was invited to and found that the young women flocked to his companion, thus relieving him of the burden of entertaining them himself. In any case, now, in Avrom's company, his thoughts were of Deborah only and flings with Washington's unmarrieds no longer interested him. He couldn't think, though, how he could use his acquaintance with Avrom to make contact with his sister. He wasn't even sure, now that she was married, that he should.

He didn't have to worry though, because it was Avrom who solved the problem. One day, several weeks after they had first met, they bumped into each other in the same canteen. Quietly and without fuss, Avrom slipped something out of his jacket pocket and placed it on the table in front of Monty. Monty recognised the writing on the envelope, addressed to him, care of Captain Avrom Mandelstam. Trying not to show the shaking of his hand, he just as quietly picked it up and slipped it into the pocket of his uniform tunic. They chatted and ate, as if it hadn't happened. All the time though, Monty was hoping they could finish and he could get back to his office.

Jerusalem
June 30, 1986

Dear Monty

Avrom has told me about meeting you in Washington and now I think it is OK to write to you.

First, let me explain what happened all that time ago, and why I have not written before. When I arrived with Rosie back at Heathrow airport, I was met by a woman who said she was from your government. She didn't say more than that but I realised what that meant. She handed me over to a Mossad agent and he escorted me on the flight to Tel Aviv. I didn't understand what it was all about but he told me on the plane that I should have nothing more to do with you, and that your own people would stop any letters getting through from me anyway. I couldn't see why everyone was making such a fuss. It wasn't as if Israel was at war with Britain, was it?

Anyway, what choice did I have? I could do nothing that might possibly affect the security of my country, and they convinced me that my relationship with you could do that. I didn't think being with you posed a security risk, but since, as they said, any letters would not get through, I didn't write. I got your letters of course, but I didn't dare reply. That's why I got my father to write to you.

So I'm sorry. It wasn't your fault, and please don't think I was angry with you. I loved our holiday together and I loved your little girl. Please do write and tell me about her. She must have grown up a lot. And what are you doing in Washington? There is so much to ask.

I expect you know I am now married. I met Dovid when he was a patient at the hospital. He had been wounded (only slightly, thankfully) interviewing some soldiers out on a patrol. I don't know why, but perhaps it was just the right moment for both of us. He had been divorced for some time and I think he was a bit down, and perhaps taking unnecessary risks. I forgot to tell you, he's a journalist. He works for The Jerusalem Post and also does some freelance work for Time Magazine and one or two US newspapers occasionally. He is quite a critic of government policy here and is quick to write

something negative about them if he doesn't agree with what they're are doing, like in Lebanon. At first I bowed to his superior knowledge in these things, but now I'm not so sure.

Anyway, it is a good marriage and I am determined to make the best of it. Dovid is not Issy (he's not you either). Everyone is different and I respect him for what he is - a good man, one who loves me and cares for me and our child. Yes, I have a daughter too, like you. Her name is Yael, after Dovid's late grandmother. She is nearly five now. If you like, I will send you a photograph of her.

Dear Monty - I do hope you can accept what has happened. It is for the best. I understand from Avrom that you have not remarried, which is a shame. You are a lovely man and some lovely woman out there must make you happy. Perhaps one of those beautiful American girls Avi tells me about!

If you are happy about it, I want you to write to me, and I will reply. I see no harm in that. After all, we are very old friends now, aren't we? I haven't told Dovid about you yet. I'm not sure how he would feel and I see no reason to upset him.

With best wishes

Deborah Kapuchinski

Washington DC
16th July 1986

Dear Deborah

I got your letter today and I'm writing straight away, which tells you how delighted I am that you wrote. I cannot say with honesty that I am delighted about your marriage, but that is a purely selfish response and having told you the truth I shall continue to tell you the truth - actually I am pleased that you are happy. Your happiness is important to me and I extend to you my sincere wishes for happiness in your life with Dovid.

And you have a daughter! I cannot tell you how delighted I am about that. I could not wish for more for you. May she also bring you much joy in your life. Does she take after you or her father? Do send me a picture, please.

Your brother is quite a man isn't he? I don't know anything about his work here but he seems to carry it off with tremendous confidence. I am sure he is serving his country well. With respect to your parents, you and Avrom are both more than the sum of them. Is that what Israel does, which Europe of old could not? The image of the European Jew seems to have died with the birth of Israel, and certainly Avrom seems to belong to a different race altogether (whilst having that sensitive side to him that I recognise in you).

Is it really all right if I continue to write letters to you? I don't want to upset anything and I can't imagine Dovid would be completely happy about it. I'm a little puzzled about this, so please let me know, because if it's not all right then of course I shan't continue.

Best wishes

Monty

Jerusalem
August 20, 1986

Dear Monty

I promise you it's alright to send me letters here. On the other hand, if it worries you, give them to Avi and he will enclose them with his when he writes. He's a good boy and we hear from him regularly. My father particularly appreciates his letters, which I read out to him, his eyes are not so good now. My mother has been in the hospital with pneumonia recently.

She is quite weak now and although we got her through this time I don't think she would survive another attack.

You are probably wondering about my husband. He's a sabra - born in Israel. His parents are also sabras, and they are a bit different from us. We thank God every day for delivering us to the promised land. Dovid's life is based on the assumption that this is our land anyway, and all we ('not God') have done is take it back from those who stole it - the Turks, the British and now the Arabs. Two ways of looking at exactly the same thing.

Anyway, as you might guess, he is not someone you argue with, so I don't bother. There is a strong feeling in this country that we have a God-given right to this land, and I don't disagree with that, but I just think we need to treat the Arabs with some sympathy. It might not have been their country before ours, but they shared it with us and I don't see why they can't continue to do so. Dovid says this is nonsense, that the Arabs were given the chance to share it when the UN partitioned British Palestine, and they turned it down because they wanted the whole country. Perhaps he's right. All I know is I see the wounded coming into the hospital and wonder how much longer we have to fight these people.

The only person who can argue with Dovid is Avi. Dovid seems to respect him, although my brother is quite a lot younger. Perhaps it's because of his job in the army - Avi knows more than most people about what's going on. I sometimes think in fact that Dovid knows more about Avi's job than I do. Anyway, when the two of them get together I just sit and listen to them. I think Avi brings out the better side of my husband.

I think too that Avi brings out the better side of you. I'm glad he has helped to bring you out of yourself. He's a great socialiser - everyone wants to be in his company. Just one thing though. I am pleased that you are there for him also. Will you look after him for me? I worry sometimes he is a bit reckless, and perhaps an older man is a good influence on him.

By the way, I don't have a picture of Yael yet I can send you. Perhaps next time.

Yours

Deborah

Washington DC
8th September 1986

Dear Deborah

I'm sending this letter back with Avrom. He has been recalled to Israel - he hasn't told me why. It might just be a briefing. He says he'll be back very soon but in my experience of army life if there's one thing you can't say it's where they'll send you next. I do hope he does return. I shall miss his company.

I'm taking some leave myself back in Britain. I haven't seen Rosie for months. I had hoped she would come out here during the school holidays but I was called away unexpectedly to go with the Ambassador to brief the Prime Minister who was over here to meet the President. In the end I had to actually attend one of the meetings at the White House, which was a very interesting experience but still I was terribly disappointed and I know Rosie was, although she tried to hide it, but what can you do when you get an order like that? Sometimes I resent being an army officer, at everyone's beck and call. Perhaps I should be back with my regiment (do I still have a regiment?) doing some real soldiering. Sorry - I'm feeling just a little sorry for myself at the moment.

If Avrom does come back I shall try to look out for him, as you ask, but to be honest I don't know much about his life here other than what he shows me, so there's probably nothing I can do.

Before he went he got a speeding ticket and wasn't going to pay the fine, partly because he genuinely didn't believe he had been speeding. I have diplomatic immunity but he doesn't, and I advised him to pay up and not cause trouble, so he did. It was a small thing, but he has to learn not to fight small battles and focus on the big ones.

I read about your husband with interest. He sounds like a forceful character (you might say rather unlike me). Anyway, we English don't say what we think, and I suspect he does just that, so perhaps I shouldn't get on too well with him, not that I'm very likely to get the chance to find out.

You are also pretty strong-willed and sure of yourself. I imagine that might cause some friction. It doesn't sound like you to give in to someone else's opinions that easily. You must have changed. Perhaps it's motherhood. Do tell me more about Yael, and don't forget a picture next time.

Yours
Monty

Jerusalem
October 24, 1986

Dear Monty

Avi gave me your letter when I saw him recently. He didn't come and see us immediately - there was something going on at the Ministry here and he was involved. Anyway, he was full of enthusiasm about you, so I think you have made a good impression on him. He instinctively didn't talk to Dovid about you. I don't think he is hiding anything but just being discreet. I have assured him there is absolutely nothing going on between us, and he trusts me. Anyway, how could there be? How many years is it since we have even seen each other? Too many.

Unusually, he and Dovid haven't had any of their long discussions this time. Avi isn't talking at all about his work in Washington and I think there are things he doesn't want us to know. I know my brother and I can tell when he is being secretive. The less he says though, the more Dovid tries to find out - that's because he's a journalist and can't resist a secret.

I think the person most pleased to see Avi was Yael. She adores her uncle and insists on holding his hand everywhere they go, and he loves her too. I think it's time he was thinking about getting married and having children of his own. He would be a wonderful husband and father.

And what about you? When are you going to meet someone nice and settle down again? I have heard about these women chasing you - it's time to slow down and let one of them catch you! Seriously, I think you should be married Monty. I can recommend it.

So what do you think of my daughter? Isn't she a beauty? As you see from the photograph, my husband is not a beauty, so it sounds terrible but I think she takes after me. My mother is not in the picture. She is in hospital again and her condition is getting worse. You will see too that my father is now an old man. I think he worries about my mother and that makes him older. Actually, from my memory of my mother as a younger woman I should say Yael takes after her.

While Avi is here and you can't send your letters with his, it might be better if you write to me at the hospital. I don't think Dovid would mind, but even so.

Yours

Deborah

Woking
26th November 1986

Dear Deborah

As you can see, I am writing to you from England. Rosie is on half-term holiday and we are spending a week at my father's house, which is made even better by the fact that he is himself away on holiday in Cyprus. Since my mother died he has gone back to his old army ways - keeping on the move. Perhaps he doesn't want to be here on his own. Actually it's a shame for him because he had booked the holiday before I knew I was coming back. I am sure he would have like to see me and he is always pleased to be with Rosie.

She has grown up dramatically since I left for America. She seems more independent than ever, which is nice but also, as a father, a bit sad. I spoke with her headmistress and she warned me not to assume Rosie is as grown up as she makes out, that some of it is her way of reassuring me that it's OK to go off and leave her. That only made me feel even more guilty.

I was sorry to read your mother is ill again. I do wish her the best, even though she doesn't know me. Do let me know how she is. By the time you get this I shall be back in Washington, so write to me there.

Yours

Monty

Jerusalem
January 11, 1987

Dear Monty

I haven't written for a little while and I am afraid I have to tell you the reason is that my mother died, on 14th December.

To be more honest, I didn't want to write, at first. I don't know if I can explain to you how I feel. Many of my friends say the same as me - that they love their mother but can't get on with her. We certainly had our differences, and I confess there were times when I wished, well that I didn't have a mother. I suppose most daughters wish that sometimes. And now I don't, and I wish I did. Was it like that when your mother died?

So now I feel bad because she's gone, and guilty because I didn't love her enough. I felt sorrow for her more than love. After what she went through, leaving Poland, then on Cyprus and losing my father, we feel pity, we all do here for people who went through the Shoah (what you call the Holocaust). I feel pity for the patients in the hospital when they die, and for their families, but that's not the same as love, is it? I know I'm supposed to love them, but I don't. And all the years with my mother I knew I was supposed to love her, but it wasn't real love. I think perhaps, when I was a child anyway, it was need. And that develops into love, or we call it that. Perhaps that's all love is. Hey, ignore me, I'm rambling.

We have a period of mourning, when it is not possible to write. My father has taken it worse than I expected.

Isn't it strange, you know someone is going to die but when it actually happens it still comes as a shock. He has gone into some kind of shell. I don't think he believes she has gone. After we arrived in Israel, and he lost her and then found her again, he became more devoted to her than he had been before. To be honest, I don't think he knew how to cope in a strange country without her. He only speaks poor Hebrew - she dealt with things like government departments and pensions and so on. I look at him and I think what his eyes tell me is that he is going to find her again, like before. I've tried telling him this time he won't.

Well, now she has gone and we are without her. It is going to be hard for all of us to make that adjustment. Avi was away with his unit, I think up in the Golan, but he returned immediately he heard and was here for the funeral. Dovid, unfortunately, was in Paris on an assignment and couldn't get back in time. I have seen a change in Avi. In a way, he now feels like the man of the family, because my father needs someone to be. It's nonsense really, because I don't live with them, and Avi himself is away such a lot, but it's something he has taken on instinctively.

I go over to see my father when I can, but with my job, and a husband and child, that's not easy. Yael is at school now, but someone has to pick her up at the end of the day. If I can't do it because of my shift, Dovid goes, but of course with his work he can't predict where he is going to be, so sometimes the school look after her until the evening, which is OK because a lot of parents are like us. That's what Israel is like. Everyone works hard and the children have to be looked after by someone.

So I am sorry to write with bad news, but that is inevitable sometimes, isn't it? Meanwhile, I hope you had a good holiday in England, and that Rosie is well.

Yours

Deborah

Washington DC
29th January 1987

Dear Deborah

I am so sorry to hear about the death of your mother. As you say, it comes as a shock no matter how expected. It was the same when my own mother died.

Please give my best wishes to Avrom, and perhaps to your father. I'll write again soon.

Yours

Monty

Washington DC
18th February 1987

Dear Deborah

I'm writing just to let you know Avrom arrived here safely yesterday. He seems a little older and more sober than before - is that because of your mother? I expect so.

I've invited him out for dinner tonight to introduce him to Julia. I know I haven't told you about her - I was going to before but it didn't seem like the right time after you had written about your mother's death. Her full name is Julia Kurtanjek and her father is Wladek Kurtanjek, the Chairman of KTX Industries, a big name in armaments here. I met her through her father, naturally, and he seems to like the idea of his daughter being involved with a British Army officer.

Anyway, for the moment, that's all it is, but I have to say I think this time it might go further. I'll let you know, shall I?

Love

Monty

Jerusalem
March 12, 1987

Dear Monty

Oho, so it's Julia is it? And how long has this been going on, without telling me? And what, exactly, does 'involved' mean? Did I say you could get involved?

Your old friend

Deborah

Washington
25th March 1987

Dear Deborah

Not only did you say I could get involved but you positively keep telling me to. You have only yourself to blame. Don't say I haven't waited for you, but you keep marrying other men, I can't wait for ever you know.

Seriously, I think you would like her. Her family are from Poland, like yours, so I guess you have something in common. Avrom has taken to her. I think actually he's a little jealous, not that with his record with women he has any cause to be. Would you like me to send you a photograph

Love

Monty

Jerusalem
April 16, 1987

My dear innocent Monty

You can send me a photograph of your Julia if you really want to. What on Earth makes you think we have something in common? Her surname isn't a Jewish one, which almost certainly makes her Catholic. I can assure you her Catholic Polish ancestry has nothing whatever in common with my Jewish Polish ancestry, and if you knew more history you would be ashamed to make such a suggestion.

So her Daddy sells weapons, does he? I'm sure you and he have a lot to talk about. Why don't you marry her and you'll be his son-in-law and then maybe one day you will inherit his factories.

Your very old friend

Deborah

Washington
5th May 1987

Dear Deborah

Old man Kurtanjek has plenty of other people to leave his factories to before me. And anyway, who said anything whatever about marriage? Forgive me saying so, but you're beginning to sound a little hysterical.

Love

Monty

Jerusalem
May 28, 1987

Dear Monty

Hysterical? Me? A less hysterical woman you won't meet in a long time. Unlike you. You're getting paranoid. What are you feeling guilty about? You don't have to you know.

Love

Deborah

Washington DC
12th June 1987

Dear Deborah

I don't feel guilty.

Love

Monty

Jerusalem
June 27, 1987

Dear Monty

What a waster you are. All that money for a stamp and apart from Dear Deborah, Love Monty, what do I get? Four words. Not even a photograph, which I remind you you did promise me. I would like to see the woman who could finally prise Colonel Montgomery Sutherland out of his cave.

Love

Deborah

Washington
14th July 1987

Dear Deborah

Here is a photograph. I am sure you can see which is Julia. It was taken at her parent's house on the occasion of the party they threw for our engagement.

We're getting married at the end of August. It's a bit rushed, but I wanted to do it before the beginning of Rosie's new school year, so she could come out. She and my father are coming the week before. Avrom has very kindly consented to be my best man, although I don't think he understands what that is. Don't you have one at your weddings? As Julia is a Catholic and I'm not, it will be a Register Office wedding, but I have agreed to a service to bless the marriage in her church.

Write and tell me you're happy.

Yours

Monty

Jerusalem
August 11, 1987

Dear Monty

Just as you were happy for me when I married Dovid, so I am happy for you and Julia. I wish you both much joy and comfort with each other. I think Avrom will tell me all about the wedding, but I don't think it is right for you to write to me again.

Your friendship over the years has meant more to me than I can tell you. I have, in my own way, always loved you, and now I love you enough to want you to be happy with someone else. Could we have had that with each other? We will never know, and now it doesn't matter. Life does that doesn't it Throws you around and leaves you where you never expected to be. Well, you have finally landed, and the very best of luck to you. Please also give my best wishes to your daughter. I am sure she is happy for you too.

With my best wishes

Deborah Kapuchinski

summer break. At the end of August the Secretary-General was travelling to Geneva and asked Monty to go with him. He took the opportunity to fly back to London with Rosie, where he met his father who was to take her on to her school. Monty flew on to Geneva, to a conference on the provision of emergency medicine in certain African states by the World Health Organisation.

Monty was booked to give the conference an assessment of the security requirements for UN staff. That evening, as he sat in his hotel room going over his paperwork before retiring, he happened to pick up the conference agenda and, without knowing why, he ran his eye down the list of speakers. Half way down the page he stopped, unable to quite comprehend what he was reading - 'The treatment of civilians in a war zone', by Dr Deborah Kapuchinski, Head of Emergency Medicine, Hadassah Hospital, Jerusalem, Israel.

I can only imagine how he must have felt. To know that Deborah was there, right there in Geneva, probably even in the same hotel. That somewhere, in that very building, she was asleep. The thoughts must have been overwhelming. That he was going to see her the next day, hear her. Possibly even meet her. If he bumped into her, say in the hospitality suite, he would have, of course, to say something. Where do you begin, with other people milling around, wanting to say things you can't?

Then another thought occurred to him. Did she know he was there? Had she seen his name on the list? He frantically looked for the agenda for his part of the conference to check he was listed. He was. Had she seen? Was she lying in bed, in a room somewhere in this hotel, thinking about him? If she did know, would she deliberately avoid him, avoid any embarrassment?

Monty didn't look at his best the next morning when he did the customary check of his uniform in the mirror, before going down to breakfast. For some reason it hadn't occurred to him that she might be in the breakfast room, but she was. She wasn't on her own though. She was sitting at a table, surrounded by people Monty could only assume to be doctors. Certainly some of them looked like Israelis, so he could only imagine she was with a group of colleagues. There was no way he could approach her, so he skirted round the edge of the room to find a free table. But Monty was over six feet of British Army colonel. He wasn't easy to hide, and in any case Deborah had been looking out for him.

Their eyes met, as they say, across a crowded room. Monty stopped involuntarily, and Deborah's intense look caught the attention of one of her colleagues, who followed her gaze and spotted Monty staring at her. Was it her husband? He might be accompanying her as a journalist, or even just for the trip. Monty forced himself to look away and without knowing how, he found a table, sat down and hid his face behind the menu.

Monty tried, in his memoirs, to express his feelings at that moment, but as I read them I found it easier to let my imagination conjure a picture for me of the scene. It seems almost like the stuff of comedy, and yet I don't suppose it felt like that to him at the time, or to Deborah.

In the event both of them were busy that first day of the conference, networking, socialising, just being (or perhaps keeping) busy, and neither was due to speak. And as it happens there was no good reason for either of them to be present in the conference chamber while the other was speaking. But they were there, both of them, listening to the other. I can only guess at whether Monty spotted Deborah in the audience when he stood up on the podium to make his presentation, and whether she saw him when she did the same. He changed into civilian clothes before returning to the WHO building for her presentation, so if she was looking for his uniform she would have been disappointed.

What I do know is that Deborah was not with her husband, that they did meet, but not until the reception on the final evening, and that they went out for dinner afterwards. Monty says in his memoirs that nothing untoward happened, and I am certain he is telling the truth. He hid nothing else, and why would he lie about this? What he actually says is that Deborah did not spend the night with him, that they did nothing which would constitute unfaithfulness.

In my experience, there is a fine line between faithful and unfaithful. I don't doubt, for example, that Julia Sutherland and Dovid Kapuchinski would have been at the very least jealous, but more likely pretty angry, if they had known that their respective spouses had spent the evening in the company of an old lover, moreover an old lover with whom they had been carrying on a correspondence for many years. I think that would constitute pretty serious grounds for concern and while one might not be able to say either had been unfaithful in body, they most certainly had been in spirit.

Loving someone who is not your spouse, someone who is married to someone else, isn't allowed. Nevertheless, how many people do it? In a way, it's the ultimate betrayal, and yet you can convince yourself you're not doing anything wrong, because the world judges faithfulness first and foremost on sexual morality. Monty and Deborah were not sexually unfaithful to their spouses and, if nothing else, they could leave Geneva the next day feeling they had, perhaps, done the right thing. If they had no control over what they felt, they had exercised control over what they did about it.

Ironically, Monty does say in his memoirs that he later regretted having been so correct, that it was an opportunity they wasted. Well, if that's how he felt with the benefit of hindsight, fair enough, but at the time both of them were sure that resisting temptation had been the right thing to do. (Even so, I only have Monty's view of the events, and he could only surmise what Deborah really felt.)

Having dinner together was an indulgence Monty and Deborah allowed themselves. The next, inevitably, was that they started writing again.

Jerusalem
September 17, 1988

Dear Monty

I find myself wondering if I imagined it. Was that you sitting opposite me in a restaurant in Geneva? Now, back home, I admit I have doubts about even writing to you. It seemed easy, there, to be someone different, but here I am me, Dr Kapuchinski, wife of Dovid, mother of Yael. Not the person you saw.

Is it possible to be both people? To be Dovid's wife and want you? I can't believe I even wrote that, but looking at the words I know they are honest. Perhaps I will never be able to tell anyone the truth, only you.

When I saw Dovid at the airport I felt, I think, two different emotions. Real pleasure, I admit. That big welcome home smile of his. Belonging. But also sadness, because now I have slipped back into this world I have lost you again.

Well, it might be wrong (OK, it IS wrong) but I'm not prepared to lose you again. I accept that we can never have what we once had, because we are both married and to ignore that would be foolish. You are happy with Julia and I am happy with Dovid. Happy? What does that mean? It's an easy word to say, but much harder to mean. I suppose the answer is that there is no definition of happiness. I guess it's relative. I'm happier than I was after Issy died, but less happy than I want to be. Oh, what a mess.

If only I hadn't met you, I could go on believing I'm

happy. Why did you have to remind me that I'm not? I'm sorry, this is all selfish nonsense. I will try to write next time with less emotion, just a chatty letter, so you don't get frightened of me.

Love

Deborah

Woking
17th September 1988

Dear Deborah

I'm just writing quickly from England before I fly back to New York. I managed to wangle a couple of days to see Rosie and my father again. Actually, I wanted to see my father for longer. I'll tell you more next time.

Love

Monty

New York
3rd October 1988

Dear Deborah

Your letter crossed with mine. It didn't frighten me - it was honest. In fact I'm glad you said those things because now I know it's all right that I feel them too. I'm sure about that.

What I'm less sure about is where we go from here. In fact I have no idea. I suppose though that the answer is obvious really. We don't go anywhere, do we? There's nowhere to go. So we stay where we are, and we write, and we write again, and one day we die. If I didn't have Rosie I can't think what I would find in life. Of course, there's Julia, but I confess being married to Julia is harder work than I thought it was going to be. What a man wants in his life is ease. Someone to come home to who brings a smile to his face at the end of the day, or in my case at the end of wherever I have been that week.

Actually, I should have said day, because my life here is pretty monotonous, just an office job really. It sounds glamorous, working for the Secretary-General, but it's like any other job. I wish I could get back to soldiering but that's all a long way behind me now. I don't suppose I could even physically do it any longer.

Anyway, I promised to tell you what I went to see my father about. Strangely, he's really an old chum of Chloe's father, but I didn't want to approach him directly. I'm going to see if he can't *pull some strings and get me something better to do than this. I'll let you know, but I don't think it's very likely.*

Love

Monty

Jerusalem
October 20, 1988

Dear Monty

Hey, don't be in a hurry to go off and get yourself killed, which I seem to remember I've had to warn you about before. I'm sure your job in New York is important. Don't forget, I heard your presentation in Geneva and you clearly know what you are talking about.

Remember Olongwe? Of course you do, but I don't mean that - I mean the breaches of security by rebels. We doctors were trying to do an important job and your commanding officer wasn't doing his. If you can make life for medical teams in Africa safer, then you are doing an important job.

I have seen such a change in you over the years. I think in Olongwe you were quite unsure of yourself (which makes me wonder if I led you on. Did I?). I don't mean to sound patronising but you have grown as you have progressed in the army. Is that why they give officers all that gold stuff on their uniforms, to give them confidence? Anyway, it does the trick for you. I was most impressed when you were on the podium - I felt proud (that's ridiculous, I know. You're not my man, so what's to be proud of?).

Now someone I do feel proud of is Avi. He's back from his wanderings around the world and, although we see soldiers every day, on the street, everywhere, Avi wears hs uniform I think with a bit more pride than most. Our officers don't seem to wear such fancy uniforms as you, but my brother still manages to impress. I know he impresses the girls (most of them are in the army). Actually there's one, she's stationed at a camp in the Negev, and he's been going down there a lot lately, so I think my little brother might be about to get hooked. He loves children (well, he certainly loves mine) and I think he would make a good husband and father. I do hope he finds happiness.

Talking of Yael, she's growing up fast. She had her seventh birthday recently. It's hard to believe it's been that long, but I suppose all parents say that. She is a great pleasure to me, although I'm not sure Dovid would say the same. He seems distracted, especially lately, and I don't think parenthood suits him. He's busy at work, but it's more than that. He has become more political since I've known him, and I'm worried about his writing - it's getting to be more what you would call liberal I think. What I mean is he seems to disagree more and more with government policy, particularly in the occupied territories, and that shows in his writing. There¹s one particular article in which he attacks them - I'll see if can find a copy and send it to you.

Well, I've been writing this in my office and I've noticed it's got dark outside. I'm going to do one more round of the emergency room, see if there are any lives that need saving with my expertise that no other doctor has! Then I'll put this in the post and go home.

So goodnight from Israel.

Love

Deborah

New York
13th November 1988

Dear Deborah

I did enjoy your last letter. I can only dimly imagine what your life is like there, so it's good when you describe it for me.

Well, my news is that I'm going to Africa! I nearly said back to Africa but this time it's the Congo. Things have been pretty bad there for the WHO teams and I'm going to see if we can stabilise the situation so they can work more safely. It was my idea, and the Secretary-General took a little persuading to let me go. He tried all the usual tricks - you know - telling me what a good job I'm doing and how he won't cope without me, but to be honest what I do is only a very small part of his responsibilities and on a day to day basis I don't suppose he even remembers who I am.

In any case, I've stuck out for this. I need to get into combat uniform again and remember what soldiering feels like. Well, it's not real soldiering, not the kind I trained for, but it's as close as I'm ever likely to get now. I'm not telling Rosie about it because she'll only worry and by the time she gets my letter and writes back I'll be back here in any case. I'm only going for a few weeks, so you can still write to me here and I'll get your letter when I return.

I've no time to write any more just now. There's kit to get ready, orders to issue, papers to arrange.

Bye for now.

Monty

Jerusalem
December 11, 1988

Dear Monty

I know you're not there but I'm writing this so you'll get it when you get back from Africa. I must say I don't really understand why you've got to go. You know, soldiers here don't go looking for trouble because it finds them without them having to. Sometimes I think you're just a boy who never grew up. I know what you're doing is important, but don't tell me there aren't other officers who can do it. You have a daughter to think of, and what would I do if you went and got yourself killed?

I'm sorry, I'm being hysterical aren't I? You won't get killed, will you?

So ignore all of that and welcome back to civilisation. And by the way, I'm off myself in a couple of days. The IDF is sending a rescue mission to Armenia to help the victims of the earthquake there last week. They asked for volunteers from the hospital and I just decided to go, I don't know why. In memory of Issy, perhaps. I shouldn't be there more than a few weeks. Dovid can look after Yael, and anyway, she's got lots of friends she can stay with if she wants - she's becoming very independent these days for one so young.

Love

Deborah

London

15th August 1989

My Dear Deborah

I am writing just as soon as possible to let you know I am all right. You probably read some of what happened in the papers, but I don't know how much would have been reported in Israel, so I'll tell you as best I can.

As soon as I got to the Congo I could see things had gone badly wrong. The government troops weren't co-operating with the UN, and the rebels were running rings round them. Without the government troops I could see we didn't have the manpower to guarantee the safety of the WHO staff, and I advised they evacuate their clinics and pull back to the capital. They argued that it wasn't necessary and that I didn't have the authority to make them do that, so I got a message back to New York and when they got a cable from the Secretary-General of the United Nations they started packing their bags.

Anyway, by this time it was too late and they were surrounded by rebel troops, and our unit lost contact with them. I'm afraid there was no choice but for me to go and confront the rebels myself. Their local commander, Capt. Chirenga, seemed a reasonable chap but I'm afraid his understanding of the truth differed somewhat from our British standards, and I found myself trapped with the WHO people. I know now that the UN officer under my command, Major Bourchier, did put together a rescue mission but that he was overruled from above. I believe my own government even considered sending an SAS team but even that was considered too risky, given the nature of the terrain and the number of WHO and UN staff being held. The potential for casualties, I believe, was too high and I think they made right decision. Major Bourchier's government did put together a company of the Foreign Legion but when they arrived I think even they could see a rescue wasn't on the cards.

As it happens the situation changed anyway. Capt. Chirenga seemed to get some instructions from his superiors and they took me to the provincial capital which they held and there I met the rebel leader, Col. Gala. I expect you've seen him in the papers, and you'll be surprised to know that he's nowhere as nasty as he looks. The amazing thing was, though, that as soon as I walked into the room we recognised each other. He was at Sandhurst at the same time as me - in fact I even taught him for a while. Well, needless to say, that changed everything. In fact I would go as far as to say, having spent quite some time with him at his headquarters, that we might be backing the wrong side in the present government. I even said so in my report when I got back but I don't suppose it made a scrap of difference. They probably thought I'd been brainwashed, which I hadn't of course. If you could hear their grievances, you would agree they have a very strong case. But Britain backs the President and that's that.

So, to cut a long story short, Col. Gala and I

went back to the clinic, all the hostages were freed, Chirenga I suspect got a bullet in the back of the head, but that's none of my business, and I shouldn't wonder from now on if WHO staff are a lot safer. So, in a rather unexpected way, I have to admit, things turned out jolly well and everyone is pleased with me back in New York and Geneva. I believe they're giving me some kind of gong, but I can't say I did a lot to deserve it.

Nonetheless, I've been shipped back here to a Ministry job again and of course Julia is here with me. The poor thing was badly affected by the whole business and wanted to me to stay in America, where she thought I would be well out of harm's reach, but she doesn't give the orders, the MoD does, and here we are. We've taken a very nice house in Hampstead on a year's lease and most days I'm in civilian clothes and look like any other commuter, which I thought I hated but actually is a bit of a relief. And being here does at least mean I get to see more of Rosie who, thank God, seems to have been oblivious of the whole episode. My father followed the whole thing in the news but thankfully kept it from her.

You can write to me here at the Ministry. Please write soon and let me know you are well. Was everything OK in Armenia? I didn't realise there was an Israeli mission - I didn't read anything in the British papers about that, as far as I remember (a lot has happened since then).

Love

Monty

Jerusalem
August 21, 1989

Dear Monty

I cannot tell you how relieved I was to get your letter this morning. I've been following what happened in the papers. The Israeli papers didn't have much about it but Dovid gets a lot of the international ones and brings them home, and I've been scanning them (without wanting to appear worried in front of him). I even thought of telephoning England but who could I ask - your father? I don't even know him. And I could hardly call New York and ask your wife, could I? And I don't suppose she knew much more than I did.

So it was very hard, not knowing. It was even worse when one of the papers said people had been killed, but I thought how could they know that, and then I realised they were probably just making it up because they didn't know anything. But I couldn't relax until I knew you were alright. Actually, you were on the television here, just briefly, a picture of you getting off the plane in New York. Dovid was with me but I just sat there watching the screen, not breathing. It was the first I knew you were safe. Luckily he didn't notice, at least I don't think he did, because he didn't say anything and he's not the sort of man to let something like that go.

He has noticed though that my mood has improved now. Things between us were getting a bit tense, and I even snapped at Yael once or twice, so the family is pleased to see Deborah back to her normal self.

Well, my dear Monty, thank God you are safe and well. Don't do that to me again. And by they way, I have looked up gong in my English-Hebrew dictionary, and I cannot imagine why the army would give you one.

Love

Deborah

London
12th September 1989

Dear Deborah

First, I must explain what a gong is. It's a word we use that you couldn't have known and it was silly of me to use it without thinking. It means a medal. The medal they are going to give me is the Distinguished Service Order, so in future I'll be Colonel Montgomery Sutherland, DSO. Impressive, huh?

I've had to tell Rosie about it, because she's coming to the award ceremony with me, but I haven't told her absolutely everything. Even so, she's made me promise that I'll stop doing silly things like getting shot at, and spend the rest of my service behind a desk, and I sort of promised.

Actually I think my old regiment (the Royal Welch Fusiliers) would like me back now I've got a high profile. Their Commanding Officer has been in touch with the Ministry and asked if they can have me but it seems I'm in demand now, so they'll have to go on the waiting list. So now I'm a distinguished soldier who's not allowed to go into battle. I'm not actually sure where that leaves me. I daresay someone else will make that decision for me - they always have done before.

By the way, I forgot to tell you, Rosie has done brilliantly in her exams and is just starting in the sixth form at school to do what we call 'A' levels. We're not at all sure where she goes after school, but apparently there is a university in

America that runs a wide range of courses for deaf students. She's looking into it, and I've said she can go if it checks out. Anyway, she's got two more years of school before that, so we have plenty of time. She's been with me quite a lot over the summer holiday, well, since I got back. I don't think she wants to let me out of her sight.

Anyway, enough about me. I do want to hear what has been happening there. I've been reading about Lebanon since I got back. Do tell me about it, because we can't get reliable news in the British Press. Is Avrom serving there

Love

Monty

Jerusalem
October 3, 1989

Dear Monty

Listen, I always thought you were distinguished anyway, so I could have told your army that and they wouldn't have had to send to Africa to prove it. Still, you've got a nice medal. Is it a nice one? I don't know what it looks like. Perhaps you should send me a photograph of you wearing it. Now I know what it is at least I won't have to imagine you wearing a gong, not that I had any idea where on your splendid uniform such a thing would have gone.

I can't tell you too much about Lebanon. There's a lot of unhappiness here about it. A lot of people are saying it's time to get out and why do we need to be there, but I think they are influenced by the international Press, who of course are unreliable when it comes to any news from the Middle East. Dovid has been writing a lot about it lately and he's part of a group of journalists who are determined to challenge the government over Lebanon.

At the hospital I talk to other people, doctors and other staff and surprisingly they have a more reasoned view of it. We think that until Israel is safe from the terrorists based in Lebanon we have to stay there. The thing I don't understand is how the international Press can complain about Israeli occupation of southern Lebanon but completely ignore the fact the Syria occupies the rest of the country. We're in the south for an obvious reason - that's where the attacks come from, but why is Syria occupying the rest of the country? I've asked Dovid that and he never gives me a straight answer. I've asked Avi as well, but he doesn't say much. He's been away a lot recently and I suspect that's where he's been. Of course, he's not allowed to tell me these things, even though I am his sister. Still, when he goes away it gives me someone else to worry about, now I don't have to worry about you. Is that the woman's lot - to stay at home and worry about her men? And how come, in that case, the one man I don't have to worry about, who has never put himself in the line of fire, is my husband?

Well, lots of questions and few answers. That's life. Oh, and mazal tov to Rosie on her success at school. Tell me more about her. Where is this university you mention?

Love

Deborah

London
30th October 1989

Dear Deborah

Some news at last! They've decided what they want to do with me. It's a posting here in London, but it is at last a real job. I'm moving over to the Department of Defence Procurement - it's the part of the Ministry of Defence that buys everything our armed forces need. It sounds like a boring job, and at the bottom end I suppose it is, but as a Colonel I only get the interesting bits. I'll be working with manufacturers on specifications for new weapons systems (just Army, not Navy or Air Force, which I don't know anything about) and advising the Minister on long-term planning for equipment.

OK, I know it's not real soldiering, but I did promise Rosie I wouldn't put myself in the line of fire, as you say, and this seems to be the best option. It's certainly a good career move. I'll be reporting directly to a Major-General and he reports to the Head of the Department, no less than an Admiral, so you could say I'll be moving in the right circles.

Thank you for your explanation about Lebanon. Actually, I brought the subject up at a mess dinner last week and even my fellow officers were ignorant about the Syrian occupation. How is that possible? Anyway, you tell Avrom to take care up there (if that's where he is, which I'm not supposed to know, am I?) and give him my best *wishes.*

I must tell you before I sign off about a funny thing that happened. I was with Rosie recently and we got talking somehow about the holiday in Cyprus, all those years ago. She remembered it, which didn't surprise me, but she also remembered you, and asked me how you are. I didn't know whether I should answer that question, how she views me being married to Julia and what she would think if she knew I was writing to you. I told her a half truth, that I know your brother through my work and he tells me your news. I don't like lying to my own daughter, but I didn't feel too bad about telling her that. I think she must have a happy memory of you. I do.

Love

Monty

London
6th November 1989

Dear Deborah

Change of plan, well a small one. The day after I wrote to you there was a call from Washington. Julia's father has been taken ill - a minor stroke they think. Anyway, she went straight out the next day and two days later rang to say the old man was asking for me. At first I couldn't imagine what he wanted me for and tried to get out of it. I can't say I have much interest in him. I've always found him somewhat abrasive and not a little arrogant. Anyway, he is my father-in-law and I didn't want to push it too far, so I've taken some leave (there always seems to be some owing to me, and it's not a bad time to be taking it before I take up my new post) and I'm flying over tomorrow. I thought I would just write today and let you know.

Love

Monty

Washington DC
11th November 1989

Dear Deborah

I'm writing from here because something strange has happened. It has been confirmed it was a stroke Julia's father had and of course she is very worried. He's had a bit of a shock himself but he asked me to go straight to the hospital when I arrived. I couldn't think what was so urgent (unless he wanted to leave me all his money, which sadly turned out not to be the case) but I did as I was asked, and Julia met me there. His speech is affected but the old so-and-so is so arrogant that doesn't stop him telling everyone what he wants. And what he wants from me is that I come and work for him. He wants me to resign my commission and take up a job at KTX Industries. He's offering me a job as Vice President - in charge of liaison with buyers (a sort of glorified salesman), so I would be doing the exact opposite of the job in Defence Procurement at the Ministry in London. The old man seems to think I've got all the right contacts. Anyway, there's a salary three times what I get paid now, and of course Julia is desperate for me to take it. It would mean of course we would live here, so I would see less of Rosie, but strangely, you remember that university I mentioned, well it's here, right here in Washington. Don't ask me how such strange coincidences happen.

Actually I don't have much experience of the

sort of thing KTX makes. It's mostly components, particularly fuses and detonators for munitions. Most of the missiles in the US arsenal have KTX components and they even make parts for nuclear weapons, though they don't talk much about that.

In any case, I haven't promised anything, except that I will consider it. Julia's got a brother and an older sister. I don't think old Kurtanjek would consider making her sister a Vice President but the brother is already in the business and I guess, as the family are the majority shareholders between them it means he will take over if anything happens to his father. I haven't had much to do with Wladek Jnr but he's one reason for not taking the job from what I have seen of him, if it means working for him one day.

To be honest, after the initial excitement of the offer, I'm not at all sure about it. It's a lot of money, and it would make Julia terribly happy (which I would like for her) but would it make me happy? I've told them I'll go back to England and give it serious thought. My feelings are that I'll take up the Defence Procurement post and see how things turn out. After all, there's no hurry. I can always come and work here another time, say in a year or two, when (if) Rosie comes to the university.

I think, writing this, I've just decided that's what I'll do, so thank you for listening!

Love

Monty

Jerusalem
November 22, 1989

Dear Monty

What can I say? No sooner do you get a gong than you get the offer of a wonderful job. Then you turn it down. Will I ever understand you? It doesn't make much difference to me where you live - since I never see you anyway.

It seems like a good opportunity, especially if Rosie does go to university in Washington. But, if I am allowed to offer an opinion, I don't think I see you doing that. I know I have only ever known you in the army, and perhaps that is all it is, but to me you are a soldier, even one who doesn't fight any longer, but still a soldier.

Actually, I asked Avi about this KTX Industries, and he didn't say much but I know him well enough to see he wasn't impressed. For Avi, that means he knows more than he is saying. I think he knows quite a lot about armaments. For a while he worked here doing the sort of thing you are doing, what you call Defense Procurement. Of course, much of the equipment the IDF buys comes from America so that's probably how he knows the company. Interestingly, I was worried about asking him because he would wonder why I was interested, but he didn't seem surprised by my question.

I can see why your wife would want you to take this up. I mean, she could live near her family, you would be earning a lot of money. Is that going to influence your final decision?

Well, my news is that I have been to Geneva again. It was strange - I didn't see you there! Seriously, I have also been offered a job. Well, not a job exactly but a position you might call it. I have written a couple of medical papers that have been used by people in the World Health Organisation and then there was the work recently in Armenia, so they have asked me to accept an advisory post with them. It will mean more work, because I will still be needed full-time at the hospital. I thought when I became Head of Emergency Medicine it would mean I would be giving other people work to do, but it doesn't seem to happen like that.

So now I will be working about eight days a week. Dovid isn't happy but to be honest I'm not especially happy with him at the moment. His articles are becoming increasingly what you might call liberal, or left-wing, I'm not sure. He has even fallen out with Avi over Lebanon. Yael is also becoming a little more in need of my attention, so it's not an easy decision to take on more work, but I have a career and I believe I owe it to myself not to slow that down for other people, even my own daughter. Anyway, we are taking some time soon for a holiday, so I hope we will all calm down a little and become a family again.

That's all my news for now, so do write soon and tell me what is happening there.

Love

Deborah

London
8th December 1989

Dear Deborah

I know I shouldn't say this, but I do wish I could see you. Don't get me wrong - it's just that I'm in a quandary and it would be good to talk things through with you.

I've come straight back to the Defence Procurement job and I thought that was it, but apparently it isn't. Julia is still over in Washington and she's been phoning every day and putting me under pressure about working for her father.

On the one hand, I don't want to to work for him, or anyone in the Kurtanjek family, but on the other it seems foolish to turn up the opportunity to have the life that it would bring, not to mention making Julia happy. And of course, as you pointed out, if Rosie does go to the university there, it makes even more sense.

So why am I hesitating? I suppose another factor is that I am institutionalised. I've been in the Army for so long it's hard to imagine a life outside it. Is that lazy of me? Why am I scared to make that leap? No, not scared, that would be putting it too strongly. No, now I think about it there's a different answer. It's not so much that I don't want to be a civilian, it's that I love the Army. Well, I've said it now, but it's true. It suits me very well. I grew up in the Army, in Cyprus and then back here with my father, and I've *never known anything else, so a psychologist would tell me I'm afraid to leave the nest but it is more than that. I actually enjoy the Army. OK, I don't do any soldiering, but that's not what I get out of it. Belonging to something that I respect and that gives me respect has value to me. And I don't think I'm ready to throw that away. Not for a salary three times what the government pays me. Not to make my wife happy. Actually, when I put it like that it makes my decision sound stupid, doesn't it? Oh well, I'll go away and think about it again and write you an equally long and pointless letter when I change my mind all over again.*

Yours

Monty

Jerusalem
December 25, 1989

Dear Monty

My goodness, you're confused aren't you? I thought being a colonel you would be capable of making quick decisions, but that apparently only applies to other people's lives. When it comes to your own, you're no more decisive than us mortals.

Listen, if you want my advice (and I think you do), do what I do, which is nothing. In my experience, it's doing things that gets you into trouble, whereas doing nothing never got anyone into trouble. You've got a job you obviously completely enjoy, and KTX Industries isn't going to go away, so you have time to think about it some more. If you leave the army and work for them and it doesn't work out, you can't go backwards (you call that burning your something, but I can't remember what). Also, I don't know your father-in-law but I suspect he will have more respect for you if you make him wait.

Have I given you the right advice? Is it what you wanted to hear?

Love

Deborah

London
9th January 1990

Dear Deborah

First, Happy New Year! (Do you celebrate it there?) And it's bridges that you burn (you asked what you burn when there's no turning back, remember?) Well, I burned mine - with KTX, not the Army. Julia was back over Christmas and we had it with my father and Rosie and generally everyone had a good time, but in the end I told Julia I had decided to stay. She was disappointed but not as disappointed as I thought she would be. I suspect she had always thought I wouldn't go. Anyway, it seems to have made her feel more settled and hopefully she won't be flying back and forth across the Atlantic so much in future.

I know we can't talk but these letters mean a lot to me and I do feel you are a friend I can talk to. Actually, talking about talking, I know it's daring but is it ever possible to really talk with you - by phone I mean? There would be no problem from my end, because my office is secure (it's what you get in this job) but is it possible from the hospital? I guess you have an office which is private. If you think we could, my number is .... [Editor's note. I have deleted the number on request, as it is still in use by the MoD.]

Having said that, I shall be travelling quite a lot, as I shall have to visit the companies we work with on new weapons systems, and they are in most parts of the world, not least good old America.

So I'm here for the foreseeable future, which in the Army isn't always as long as you think it's going to be.

And by the way, I nearly forgot to tell you. I bumped into Avrom again, of all places at the Ministry. I don't know what that brother of yours gets up to but first he's at the Pentagon and now he's here. I can't ask him straight out what he's doing and, in any case, I don't need to tell you what he's like. He wouldn't tell me, but by the time he's finished not telling me I would have forgotten what I wanted to know in the first place. He has what we call the gift of the gab. Anyway, we had dinner together at my home last night. Julia was unhappy with me for inviting him, not least, sadly, when I told her he is Jewish, but Avrom isn't one to let a little racial prejudice get in the way. He was charming to Julia and she responded as expected by being gracious to him, even I suspect flirting a little. After half an hour she quite forgot where he comes from. Your country should use him as an ambassador.

Call me.

Love

Monty

Jerusalem
January 24, 1990

Dear Monty

How strange to hear your voice. I'm still not sure how it feels, to be able to pick up the telephone and just call you. Lovely, actually. I'm still a bit dazed by it, and it makes me wonder why we haven't done it before. It also makes me feel just a little guilty. I'm married and so are you. As long as we write, it doesn't seem wrong, I don't know why, but it doesn't. But talking with you seems, well, a bit more like being unfaithful (actually, being unfaithful right now feels like fun, with you I mean of course. But I shouldn't say that, should I?)

Actually, I didn't like that secretary of yours. Is she a soldier? I had the feeling she wanted to know exactly what I wanted you for before she would put me through. Listen, if I told her what I wanted you for you could have got into a lot of trouble (but I'm not supposed to say that either, am I?). I think if I'm going to ring again I had better make up some name, you know, pretend to be from some armaments company in some country where they have foreign accents that she wouldn't know from Israeli ones. No, next time I'll put on my best American accent, that will fool her. It might even fool you. Does she know your wife?

I'm glad you've met up with Avi, and I'm not surprised your wife gave in to his charms. Here's a thought - why don't we get the two of them together and then ..... no I really must stop saying things like that.

As you can tell, talking to you has made me go all girlish. I don't know if that's a good thing or a bad thing.

Seriously, do you remember I once asked you to look after Avi? Well, can I say that again? He thinks he's awfully clever and that he will always be able to get himself out of scrapes but one day he's not going to. If you happen to be there at the time, I'm sure I can depend on you to help him. I know you probably couldn't do anything, and you don't know anything about his work, but as you can tell I worry about him and he's there and you're there so it seems like a sensible thing to ask, which it probably isn't at all.

I'll try to resist the temptation to keep phoning you.

Love

Deborah

London
12th February 1990

Dear Deborah

So the great Dr Deborah Kapuchinski, Head of Emergency Medicine, can be girlish. I bet your staff never see that side of you. Does your husband?

It was wonderful talking to you. We shouldn't do it too often though. My 'secretary', as you call her, is Private Gummer and I'm not entirely sure if she's here to look after me or to watch over me (after Northern Ireland I question everything, and everyone, but I'm probably being paranoid). In any case, I can call you from time to time but it's probably better if you only call my office very occasionally, so she doesn't start to recognise your voice.

As it happens I shall be out of the country for a while. I can't say too much, but it's to do with the kind of equipment I was using in Northern Ireland (listening equipment, that's all I can say). I'll write again when I get back.

Love

Monty

PS. Mark your letters 'Private and Confidential', just to be on the safe side, and don't write until I get back.

As he thought it would be, it was a while before Monty was able to write again. This is the first indication we get, either from his letters or his memoirs, that his job in Defence Procurement involved more than just the mundane purchase of military equipment. I can say now what he could not say to Deborah at the time, that his work in Northern Ireland had involved clandestine surveillance and what he did at the Ministry was connected with the experience he had with specialist equipment in that field. (I think it probably also was a factor when he decided not to go to work for KTX Industries, whose speciality was quite unconnected with his.)

His trip took him to the USA and Greenland, where the US military was installing satellite tracking and monitoring equipment and I know he made a number of flights with UK colleagues from the USAF airbase at Keflavik, but even his memoirs are shy of saying precisely what equipment he was working on. It is public knowledge though that Britain and America were jointly developing the Aurora Project at that time, and that a number of British companies, including the SRL-British Military Technologies Group consortium, were heavily involved in that project.

Much of Monty's work since joining the department had been with BMT Group, and one of their directors, General Sir James Bowden, had been his commanding officer in the Royal Welch Fusiliers before retiring and taking a plum job in the armaments industry. General Bowden was an occasional guest still in Monty's mess and had dined at the Sutherland house on one occasion. Although his rank was higher than most of the men who got invited to these dinners, the two got on well together and his presence in his house was something of a coup for Monty. There were other dinners, rather more informal, to which Avrom Mandelstam was invited, but the two groups of people did not meet, at least never under Monty's hospitality.

Just then, however, there was little time for entertaining. The Aurora Project was running both behind schedule and over budget, to add to which it didn't work. As Monty said in his memoirs with his typical muted sarcasm, 'Another triumph of British technological ingenuity'. He was right in that the problems were on our side, and the Americans were getting worried and not a little critical of their partners. He had to make a number of trips to Washington, where he still had a good reputation, to attempt to smooth things over. He also made a number of visits to the headquarters of British Military Technologies where he made quite clear the concerns of his employer, the British Government.

While this was going on either he didn't give much thought to Deborah or he simply didn't have the time to write, I don't know. It was more than six months before she got another letter from him. Following his instruction, she had not written meanwhile.

Jerusalem
April 30, 1990

Dear Monty

I'm sorry to read that your wife has been unwell. It's nothing too serious I hope?

I hope also that your holiday was good. I remember the first time you told me about the house in France - that was when you got together with Chloe, wasn't it? Perhaps that's why you and Julia have never been there together. And how is Rosie? Do write and tell me about her. Are her studies going well, and has any decision been made about university?

I won't ask you about where you've been. I know enough from Avi's work not to ask too many questions. My work, of course, is just very dull, you know, saving people's lives, that sort of thing. Well , not even that so much now, more paperwork and meetings than anything. Like you, I don't often get away from my desk nowadays.

One thing I must tell you about is a very exciting project I'm involved in. Some old friends of Issy's, mostly from medical school, recently had a reunion and I don't know who started the idea but they have established a medical scholarship in his name. It will be for an African student to come here to study at our medical school. It's called the Dr Issy Bar-On Scholarship (unsurprisingly), and naturally I'm a trustee. We're doing fund-raising here and in America and so far we have enough for the complete course for the first student. I'm even hoping we might be able to support two eventually, but we'll have to see if the donations keep coming. I might even see if I can squeeze some money out of my colleagues at WHO.

I'm sending you a photograph of me and Yael, so you can see how she is growing up. We went into Dovid's office and one of the staff photographers took it.

Actually, Avi hasn't written recently, so please tell him to get in touch with his big sister!

Love

Deborah

London
17th May 1990

Dear Deborah

Thank you for the photograph. Yael doesn't look like you, does she, so I suppose she takes after her father.

We had a super holiday. Julia loved France and she and Rosie get on quite well. They did have one argument but I think that was more to do with two women in the kitchen at the same time than anything else. They both love to cook (which suits me, because I don't) and they both I think wanted to impress me, so there was some competition. It was friendly up to a point but I did have to separate them just once.

In any case Julia was tired and I think she needed to rest more than anything. She has seen her own doctor in Washington and the Army doctor in London but no-one has suggested what the problem might be. Perhaps it will pass in time.

I haven't seen Avrom recently, not since my last letter. In fact I've asked one or two people here who also know him but no-one's saying. He's probably on some highly-secret mission. I expect we'll find out eventually (or, knowing Avrom, probably not), so don't worry. By the way, has he ever mentioned a Mr Wilson to you?

Love

Monty

This is the first mention in either the letters or his memoirs of Mr Wilson. I don't know how much Monty knew about him at that time, or what prompted him to ask if Deborah knew of any connection between him and Avrom.

When I read this letter It didn't occur to me that Mr Wilson was going to be important in this story. In fact he turned out to be very important, but I'll let the story unfold at its own pace.

What I can say is that I do detect in Monty's letter a slight concern about Mr Wilson and Avrom, but I admit that might only be with the benefit of hindsight. To the reader (Deborah of course was the first reader, and it aroused no suspicions in her) it's an innocent enough enquiry.

Jerusalem
May 31, 1990

Dear Monty

First, I want to thank you for your cheque. When I wrote about our medical scholarship I didn't mean I wanted you to make a donation. Nevertheless it is very generous and kind of you and, on reflection, I am not surprised. It did give me just a little difficulty explaining to my colleagues who you are, but I made up a story and what do they care - it's money.

How is your wife? Is she recovered? What tests have the doctors run? I'm sorry to be inquisitive, but I'm a doctor, it's what we do. It's probably nothing to worry about I expect, but still I would like you to write and tell me what's happening.

Avrom has turned up. As usual, he declined to answer any questions. Actually he explained a little about his work, perhaps more than he should have, which I can't tell you but I can say it's important. And I believe he's the right person to do it. He's dedicated to our country and I know he will do his best for us. Of course I don't want him to get hurt but our soldiers get hurt every day - that's the nature of war. I don't know why he finally decided to tell me those things I think he finds life a bit lonely sometimes. He has girlfriends, but as far as I know there has never been a serious relationship.

I haven't told my father about this. He would worry, although I think he would be proud as well, as I am. His health is not good, although he's tough and in my medical opinion he could go on for years. Perhaps he knows more than I think he does. Like me, he would like to see Avi settle down. I don't see why his work would make that impossible. Anyway, I remembered to ask him about your Mr Wilson and his reaction was surprising. He was shocked that I knew the name, but then he said he had never heard of him. My brother could probably keep a secret under torture, but can't keep one from his sister. So that's all I can tell you. I would say he does know this person, but he doesn't want me to know he does. What does that mean? Who is Mr Wilson?

I was going to talk to Dovid about this but decided not to. I'm not sure what kind of people he is mixing with these days and while I wouldn't ever accuse him of doing anything to harm Israel, I think he is naive about the motives of some people, which is surprising for a journalist with his experience. I'm sending you a piece he wrote about Lebanon and I think you will see what I mean. He's not the only person in Israel these days who thinks we should just get out, but I don't see how we can ever protect ourselves from Syria unless we protect our northern borders, and if that means occupying a small part of Lebanon then that's what we have to do. This probably doesn't mean a lot to you in England but to us it's life and death, so I'm sorry if it's not interesting.

Actually, you are such a kind man I am sure you do have an interest in my country. I wish I could talk to you properly. We can't talk for long on the telephone, certainly not about subjects like this. Maybe one day.

All my love

Deborah

London
18th June 1990

Dear Deborah

You said in your last letter that maybe one day we'll be able to see each other and talk. Well, no sooner asked than done. I shall be there on 5th July for three days.

It's not a state secret so I can tell you we are buying specialist equipment from Israel Defence Industries. I would have to go and see them at some time so it suddenly occurred to me when I read your letter that I can actually do that when I like, and I would like to do it soon. They are excellent people and to be honest there is nothing that could not be dealt with by a more junior officer in my department, but it does no harm to show some brass from time to time.

I shan't actually be in Jerusalem on business but I can easily pass through on my way to the airport, so I'll phone you nearer the time and give you the details. I don't want to make your life complicated at all but will it be possible to meet me?

Love

Monty

Jerusalem
June 25, 1990

Dear Monty

I hope this letter reaches you before you leave for Israel. Yes, whatever it takes I will find a way to see you. Call me either before you leave or once you arrive, at the hospital.

Have a safe journey.

Love

Deborah

I don't know what plans Monty and Deborah made to meet, but they were overtaken by events. At Ben Gurion airport Monty was met by a representative of Israel Defence Industries, but on the way across the concourse he bumped into Avrom - again. The man from IDI seemed quite happy to relinquish his charge to Avrom so Monty assumed the latter carried considerable weight and that his identification card meant a great deal to whoever he might want to show it to.

Avrom delivered Monty to his his hotel, where the IDI representative would pick him up in the morning and take him down to their manufacturing facility in the Negev Desert. Before Avrom left him he invited him to his apartment for dinner that evening and as tired as he was (and he was hoping to find a way of seeing Deborah) he felt he couldn't refuse, that Avrom had a reason for meeting him and that this invitation was somehow important. Monty particularly wanted to ask him about Mr Wilson, and this would be an ideal opportunity.

Yet again, though, events overtook them and the evening turned out very differently from both of their expectations. It seems that Avrom called his sister and invited her round to his apartment later that evening for coffee to meet a friend from England (did he know she would know who he meant?). Deborah's daughter, Yael, took the message and her father got to hear of it. He, innocently enough I suppose, invited himself along as well, perhaps simply because a visitor from England was always interesting to a journalist who knew or suspected a little about his brother-in-law's work. Did he find it strange that Avrom invited Deborah and not him? Perhaps that was normal given the odd hours Dovid worked, I don't really know.

So that evening an interesting group of people sat in the living room of Avrom Mandelstam's apartment: his sister the doctor, her husband the journalist with suspect political views, and the man she loved, a man moreover possibly closer to people of power in her government, at least in the military, than anyone else there.

What would I give to have been a fly on the wall that evening. For Monty and Deborah it must have been agony. Did they give anything away? Nothing subsequently suggests Dovid had any idea of their relationship but I have never been able to understand how, because these two people did love each other, of that there is no doubt, whether they loved their respective spouses or not. In a small Jerusalem apartment there could have been nowhere they might have been alone even for a minute.

This would seem an appropriate point at which to look at the whole issue of Monty and Deborah's relationship. Even to call it that might seem an exaggeration; after all, how often did they see each other, or even talk on the telephone? Do two people who write regularly have a 'relationship'? I accept that I don't know what they talked about during their infrequent telephone conversations - they might have been more intimate than the letters I suppose. My premise throughout has been that what they had could properly be called a relationship, with all that implies. Leaving aside the question of whether loving someone else's spouse is wrong, in my experience of the world people judge others by what they do, not by what they think or feel. It seems reasonable to say that two people sharing a love across an entire continent are behaving innocently. Some might even say they were, in today's parlance, a sad pair. I don't think they were. I think that is looking at them in a negative way - seeing what they didn't have instead of what they did. I think their glass was half full, not half empty. I am quite sure they were frustrated by their situation, but at the same time Monty was happy in his own way with his marriage to Julia and Deborah was fond of Dovid. And yet, there must have been dissatisfaction in their marriages because is it not true that someone who is completely happy with their partner would not concern themselves with anyone else? Or is it not that simple? I am only a humble journalist turned biographer. I'm in no position to judge.

Another way of seeing the pair was that perhaps they were greedy - that they wanted it both ways. I suspect if that were true they would have made more effort to see each other. I'm not saying they wouldn't have liked to see each other more but surely two people who were, shall we say, 'in love' would go further than they did. So I don't say they were in love, I think they loved, which is of course something different. They had been in love, remember, on Cyprus.

It's a hypothetical question, but an interesting one to ponder nevertheless, but what would they have done if they had both been free? It's a question I'm sure many people ask themselves about their own situations.

What Monty and Deborah planned to do after that evening was to find another opportunity to meet. Monty's business in Israel was finished ahead of schedule and he was about to leave the offices of Israel Defence Industries when a call was put through to him. It was from London. Julia had been taken ill.

London
21st July 1990

Dear Deborah

I'm so sorry I didn't get to see you again. I hope you got my message at the hospital. In fact Julia is not as bad as they said. She was taken to hospital and they did extensive tests, and we're waiting for the results. I am afraid you are probably right about this and I think she knows as well, or at least suspects, but neither of us is saying anything until the test results come back in the hope that we are wrong.

Meanwhile she's feeling a little stronger and she's at home recuperating. Her brother Victor has come over and he's been putting me under a little pressure to let her be flown over to the States for tests. I don't think they believe we have proper hospitals here. In fact she's been getting the very best of attention at the King Edward VII Hospital for Officers but what can they do until they know for sure what it is?

I'll keep you informed.

Love

Monty

Jerusalem
August 4, 1990

Dear Monty

Your last letter arrived the day after I spoke with you. I don't know what to say that will be a comfort to you. I'm sure the doctors there have given you their prognosis but you know Multiple Sclerosis, for all the fear the name induces, is not a death sentence. It sounds to me like she has the kind that goes into spontaneous remission and that's good. It means she will be able to live some sort of normal life, at least some of the time.

I honestly don't think there is any point her going to America for treatment. What can they do that your own doctors can't, or for that matter that we couldn't here? It's easy to understand her desire to be at home (forgive me calling it that but she must feel it's home at this time). And of course her parents would like her there, even if they did have faith in British doctors. But if the trip is going to tire her more than she already is then surely it's better she doesn't go, not yet anyway. And dare I say it but if she goes, might she be persuaded to stay there, especially as the disease progresses?

Dearest Monty, I can only assure you that you are - both - in my thoughts. If there is any advice I can give professionally, do please ask.

Your good friend

Deborah

Woking
9th October 1990

Dear Deborah

We are here in Woking at my father's house for a few days. Julia has been quite poorly for a while but she seems to be slowly improving and I thought she could recuperate in the country better than London. My father is terribly kindly towards her and there's plenty of room here. Her family wanted to pay for a full-time companion / nurse, which she really doesn't need. It would only make her seem like an invalid. There will be time for that later.

She knows what the prognosis is and I'm afraid she is pretty low at the moment - mentally, I mean. It's made me stop and think as well, about what it would be like to suddenly have your life altered that dramatically. You know, we assume certain things about life, and one of them is that it will go on much the same as it always has until we slow down through old age, which we consider quite natural. My father is certainly showing his age, but it doesn't seem strange either to me or, I think, to him. But when someone is struck down in the prime of their life - at the wrong time, as it were - well, it seems just that - wrong. Unjust, I suppose you would say, and I don't blame Julia for feeling angry about it.

Perhaps I even feel a little angry about it myself. I'm not sure what I'm angry about though. Is it anger for her, I mean an unselfish *kind of anger, or am I angry because the woman I married has been taken from me? Even writing it that does sound incredibly selfish, when I'm not the one with the disease, but I admit there is an element of that.*

I'm sorry to ramble like this. I think it helps me to write to you. There are things I wouldn't say to anyone else, not face to face. Anyway, if I may I shall write again when there is more news.

Yours

Monty

Jerusalem
November 27, 1990

Dear Monty

I'm sorry I haven't been able to write for a while, but I was busy with a study for WHO and then I had to go to Geneva to present a paper on it and then when I got back there were so many things to catch up with. I expect you understand.

I did think there would be another letter from you when I got back but you haven't written. I do hope everything is alright. Write soon and let me know.

Love

Deborah

London
8th December 1990

Dear Deborah

It's my turn to apologise. Don't worry - Julia is all right, in fact she is really rather better. I think Woking was an excellent idea. She and my father are getting on really much better than I dared hope. I don't now why, to be honest, but there you are. She has taken over as the woman of the house and he I think feels rather good about that. Oddly, despite her illness, he is letting her run things. I guess that's good for her, and for a man who has always had a wife to manage his home it's good for him as well. I confess I find it strange but at the same time a relief. It feels odd when I go down, (which I do as much as I can) because in a way they are like an old married couple and I almost feel like a visitor in their home.

Anyway, it means Julia is happy to stay there and I don't have to worry about my father feeling imposed upon. It's really very helpful because I am extremely busy in London. I've had quite a lot of time off with all of this, compassionate leave, and I need to get my head down. The safety of the nation won't wait for me!

My report on the Israel trip was well received and that project is going pretty well. They think at the Ministry that I'm a specialist in that sort of thing, so I expect I shall be back before too long. And by the way, I never got to ask Avrom what he *knows about Mr Wilson, so if you see him perhaps you would ask him yourself? Don't discuss it with anyone else though, just to be on the safe side.*

Love

Monty

Jerusalem
December 23, 1990

Dear Monty

I'm sorry to worry you but it's about this Mr Wilson. I did ask Avi, but he said I shouldn't concern myself and he seemed a bit worried that I was asking. I don't know what it's about or who he is, but the feeling I get is that unless it's a problem for you you would be best to forget about him.

These notes on MS might be of help to you. They are from an American publication. A lot of it you won't understand but the parts on the development of the disease, and how people cope with it, are quite clear.

By the way, Avi has been promoted. He's a Major now, and I'm very proud of him. He's also rather proud of himself, but that's Avi for you.

Love

Deborah

London
19th January 1991

Dear Deborah

Happy New Year! Do you celebrate it? Actually, I think I ask you that question every year. Anyway, we've had a quiet Christmas here. We all got together in Woking and Julia was really quite well, and Rosie was slightly put out that she wasn't running the house for her grandfather but she was very understanding about Julia and no-one felt like having an argument over whose kitchen it was. My father quite liked having two women to make a fuss over him. Mr and Mrs Kurtanjek came over as well but thankfully we didn't see them until Boxing Day (that's the day after Christmas) and they were only passing through anyway. I must say my father didn't take to Wladek (and my father, I can tell you, is a pretty shrewd judge of character). Still, it was great for Julia to see them, albeit briefly.

I'm back in the office now but not for long. I'll be off to Washington in a few days, and I expect to be away for a couple of weeks. I must say having Julia taken such good care of is a great relief. It means I can get on with my work with a clear conscience. I get down there most weekends but just before Christmas I received an order to prepare a report for the Commons Defence Committee and I have to present it to them as soon as I get back from the States so, as you can see, I am working flat out.

You know, with all this going on it's been a while since I've had one of your nice chatty letters. Do write a long letter and tell me everything that's going on there.

Love

Monty

Jerusalem
February 15, 1991

Dear Monty

You're right - I haven't written with any of my own news recently. I didn't feel it was appropriate with your wife's illness - I thought you would not be interested in what is happening in my life at the moment.

Of course a lot has happened, and at the time I kept thinking, 'Oh, I must tell Monty that'. But now I come to tell you it all seems very small and unimportant.

Dovid has changed his job. The paper he was working for eventually decided his articles were getting too liberal and they gave him a choice of representing their political views more closely or leaving. I hoped he would change but he said he couldn't, so he left. My next worry was the loss of his salary. Israel is an expensive country to live in and even with my pay, which is higher than most people's, we couldn't manage without his as well. Luckily, his articles in the Post had attracted some attention, even if it's the attention of the wrong people. Well, I think they are the wrong people, but of course for him they are the right ones. Another paper, a much more left-wing one, has snapped him up, although the salary is a bit lower. Anyway, he is much happier, because he can write anything he likes about the government and they will print it. I am less happy, because to be honest we have almost given up trying to agree on politics. Now he has this new job he's not listening to any arguments (not that he ever did anyway), because he knows everything there is to know and that's that.

It means that instead of the lively political arguments we used to have now we have silence.

Issy's scholarship fund is going well. The first student is already here, from Kenya. We have all been making a big fuss of him and although at first he was terribly shy and nervous I think we've done a good job because now he walks around the hospital with a big smile on his face and it's a pleasure to see. This is the first time he has been out of his country and I suppose it must seem very strange, especially the weather. Jerusalem gets quite unpleasant in the winter and we have had rain and high winds and the kind of weather you are probably used to in England. I remember you once told me I wouldn't like English weather - do you remember, when I wanted to come and live there with you? Well, I can tell you it's no better here at the moment. Ever since that time there have been moments when I have wondered what it would have been like. Not just the weather I mean - being together. Well, what is the point of wondering things like that?

Yael has been badly behaved recently. I think she senses the tension between me and Dovid and she reacts with bad behaviour. I do sometimes regret how little time I have spent with her but I will try a bit harder to find some time. I don't want things with Dovid to go wrong of course. I wouldn't go so far as to say we are the happiest couple in Israel but we do have things in common and we have a daughter who needs us, so I will try harder to be a good wife and mother.

Avi tells me he's going to England soon (which is amazing because he never usually tells me where he's going), so I expect you will see him.

Well, now you know my news. Not all of it, because mostly it's quite boring, and I don't want you to be bored with me.

Love

Deborah

London
7th March 1991

Dear Deborah

I've just finished reading your letter for the third time, sitting here at my desk. Did you know I keep your letters? I have every one of them, going back to 1970. I keep them in an old filing box that no-one would ever think to look in, and it's followed me around to my various postings. I dont suppose you keep mine.

Things have settled down to some sort of routine here. Unless I'm away I spend most of my working week here in my office or in other government departments like the Treasury. They put me here because of my specialist knowledge but to be honest the whole of government seems to me to be run by accountants, and they have no idea of what makes an army work. Sometimes I think they should be sent out to face an enemy with substandard weapons and then they might worry less about money and more about soldiers' lives. Actually, I'm not supposed to say that.

At weekends I generally get down to Woking. I've considered commuting daily from there but I don't think I could face the journey every day. In any case, I don't think Julia would know what to do with me if she had me there every evening. So I go back to the flat and live a bachelor life. Only very occasionally does it get lonely. To tell the truth, I rather like this kind of life. It makes me wonder if I was cut out for marriage at all. Well, things haven't worked out how I expected anyway and I don't live a normal married life, do I?

Some nights I take your photograph out and put it by my bed. I know you will think that's completely foolish but I am a fool, and I can't hide that from you. I suppose it's quite wrong of me but they can't hang you for a photograph, can they? I'm quite sure Julia would be devastated if she knew, but she doesn't, so I feel guilty but not as guilty as all that. Come to think of it, I don't have her photo out - now that IS worrying.

What is also worrying is that one evening I had Avrom here for a few drinks and at one point he wanted to go the bathroom, which is off my bedroom. It was only afterwards that I realised your picture was out but it's pretty unlikely he saw it. Still, he did look a bit strange when he came back, although I was probably imagining that. We talk about you sometimes and he is always too polite to ask, but how much does he know?

Come to that, how much is there to know? Do you realise we have known each other for more than twenty years? That's longer than I have known anyone else. Does that make us an old unmarried couple? Seriously, I do feel closer to you than anyone I know. How can that be? We write, and I spoke to you on the phone two months ago. So why are you so important to me? I don't expect you think of me as much as I do about you. Your life is busier than mine, and your daughter lives with you, which mine doesn't.

Well, should I tear this letter up because it's a load of 'sentimental hogwash. If you read it, *you'll know I didn't.*

Love from your very very old friend

Monty

Jerusalem
April 2, 1991

Dear Monty

Was that a love letter? Well, you've no business sending me such a thing, but I'm more pleased than I can tell you that you did, and I'm glad you didn't tear it up. Sometimes I'm not sure why you write to me. Is it just something to do when you're bored? I'm sure you must get bored stuck there in that flat on your own. Haven't you ever been tempted to go out with other women? By the way, that wasn't a suggestion.

Isn't that silly? You and I are both married to other people but I would be jealous if you had a relationship with another woman. Work that one out.

I must tell you the other day one of my colleagues, Dorit, started making comments about my marriage. She knows Dovid (he plays tennis with her boyfriend) and for no reason she said something about him. I don't know if it was said to see what my reaction would be but it worked. What she was saying hinted that Dovid is seeing someone else. I was so shocked I didn't say anything but I realised she was watching my face to see if I understood what she was saying, and I tried not to show I did. I can't be sure she was actually suggesting he is, or perhaps she just meant it as a joke. I can't explain how the conversation went to you in a letter.

That evening I watched him closely to see if there was anything different about him, but Dovid is an expert at not showing his feelings. He's so good at it sometimes I wonder how we ever got together. Not like you though - you don't really show your feelings but I have never felt you were hiding them either. Of course I have never been married to you so I can't know what you are like to live with. But with Dovid I do sometimes get the feeling he is hiding. Not hiding what he has done but hiding himself, if that makes any sense.

I could just ask him but if I do that he might tell me, and do I really want to know? And if he denies it, how will I know if he's lying, so what's the point of asking? All it would do is stir up a lot of problems. I've asked myself why I don't want to stir up problems and I think the answer is the same for everyone. We don't want our lives to change. I have my work, and Yael, and what Dovid gives me of himself, and a nice home (not maybe by your standards but for Jerusalem), and my friends and my father. If Dorit is right (and I don't even know if she was being serious), so much would change.

Does that mean I'm prepared to share him? No, not at all. It doesn't mean that, it means as long as I don't know then there is no problem. If I were being completely honest I would have to admit that I wouldn't feel like this if I really loved him, so there, I've said it, I don't. But that doesn't mean I want to end our marriage either.

Dear Monty, I know your marriage finished when your first wife had an affair, but can you understand why I have taken this attitude? In any case, you knew about her for sure. I don't know about Dovid.

I'm sorry - you wrote me such a lovely letter and all I've done is tell you bad news. Or is it?

Love

Deborah

PS. I have every one of your letters since Africa. They are hidden at the apartment in a huge pile of medical papers.

London
24th April 1991

Dear Deborah

I'm shocked that you keep my letters. Is that safe? And I'm sorry to hear about Dovid. I agree with you that it's dangerous to go too far into it, because what if he's completely innocent? Accusing him without any grounds would do a lot of damage to your marriage. On the other hand, what if it's true? I suppose the answer to that is a question. If it were true, how much would it matter to you? You probably think I want it to be true, but I don't. Regardless of my feelings for you, I don't wish that for you.

I have tried to imagine being in the same situation as you, and I can't. How do you lie next to someone in bed wondering about them? To my mind, marriage is only marriage if it is based on absolute, unconditional trust. The kind of trust you don't even have to think about because it comes naturally from love. If, as you say, you don't truly love Dovid, then the basis for that kind of marriage doesn't exist.

I think my views on marriage are inevitably informed by my marriage to Chloe, and I admit I'm no expert, so I don't know why I think I should be giving you advice. Actually, I don't mean it as advice. These are just my thoughts, and perhaps you will take them (or leave them) as such.

Paradoxically, I'm a little hurt for you, that

your husband is perhaps unfaithful. That is silly, because I want you (I hesitate, but yes, it's true, I want you) and I can't have you as long as you are happily married. I can't have you anyway because I'm also married. And I still couldn't have you because, well, to be honest I don't know if you want me, and I must assume you don't, not to that extent anyway.

I think this makes sense, and I'm going to post this letter before I get a chance to screw it up.

Love

Monty

Jerusalem
May 13, 1991

Dear Monty

I do. Want you, I mean.

Love

Deborah

When I read this letter from Deborah I couldn't help but stop and pause for reflection. I suspect you, the reader, will do the same.

Monty and Deborah had been writing for more than twenty years. They had been in and out of love, with each other and with other people. At this point I can tell you something I only found out by reading the rest of their letters. Neither of them ever fell in love with anyone again. By that I mean the love they had for each other was to last for the rest of their lives.

Finally, they have been able to say the word. I have only been able to surmise that this came about because of the confluence of events in their individual lives. Monty's wife, Julia, is fast becoming an invalid. Does that make him a bad person, not loving her enough at this time? Perhaps it does, but strangely I would say in his defence that I don't think he had ever loved Julia, not with the kind of unconditional love he talks about. I think he understood love and I believe he knew he had married Julia for some good reasons, but love (his kind of love) wasn't one of them. In fairness it should also be said that Julia probably didn't feel that unconditional love for Monty either. I don't have the advantage of a pile of correspondence from her, so she is someone I have had to a large extent to guess at.

All of this doesn't mean they were wrong to marry in the first place. Why should a marriage based on what they felt for each other not work, at some level? The answer to that is that Monty loved someone else, Deborah. Had she not already been married at the point when he and Chloe split up, who knows, perhaps he and Deborah would have got together. That's life, isn't it? You're in the right place at the wrong time, or the wrong place at the right time, but whatever and wherever you are, being in the right place at the right time is a glorious coincidence that leads to a great deal of happiness but is given to few.

And what of Deborah's life? Again, for Monty I have his memoirs - no such information exists for Deborah, although I have spoken with Yael, her daughter, and some of my understanding of this rather enigmatic woman comes from her.

As it turned out, Dovid was having an affair. I think this was more to do with the breakdown in the compatibility between him and Deborah than that he went out looking for someone else, but here I admit I am guessing. I don't think it takes a lot for someone to look for someone else outside their marriage and I don't think, contrary to popular belief it is always, or even often, about sex (or even love). It's not hard to imagine the environment Dovid found himself in, writing for a publication that leaned far to the left of Deborah's political views. He would inevitably have met many people in that environment whose views more closely matched his own. Given Deborah's long work hours, which can't have tallied much with Dovid's, it's not hard to see how they might have drifted apart. How much Deborah's feelings for Monty came into this equation is impossible to know.

I would say two things happened now to Monty and Deborah. Their relationship with each other became more secure (although I'm afraid that's not the end of the story for them by a long way). But at the same time events started to conspire against them, but especially against Monty. There were people in his life who, wittingly or otherwise, were destined to make his life difficult. There was Avrom. Until now, although Monty knew he was in the Israeli security service, probably the Mossad, it didn't occur to him that whatever Avrom's work involved concerned him. In this he turned out to be mistaken. And there was the Kurtanjek family (particularly Julia's brother, Victor) and the company they controlled, KTX Industries. Monty already had doubts about both the family and the company, but being married to the daughter of the President naturally clouded his judgment. And finally there was Mr Wilson, about more of whom in due course.

So the path of love did not run smoothly, and after more than two decades our long-distance lovers still had some waiting to do. It cannot be ignored that they were both married. Did Deborah's revelation that she no longer loved her husband change everything? No, it didn't change anything. Even his affair (which remember she was by no means sure about at this time) didn't end their marriage. And I detect in Deborah a loyalty to Dovid that, fair enough, is hard to understand if he was being unfaithful, but I have put it down to loyalty to the institution of marriage, rather than to the man in question. I think Deborah was in some ways a conventional person, and she simply didn't want her marriage to fail. On top of that, undoubtedly, was her concern for Yael. Every woman wants her children to have a father, even an imperfect one, and it can take a lot to take that relationship apart if it can reasonably be held together.

If we attribute loyalty to Deborah, so much more must we do so in the case of Monty. He didn't love his wife to the exclusion of all others, but she was a sick woman, and there can be no doubt that her illness brought out the right instincts in him. Monty stuck with Julia to the end. One inevitable consequence, though, of their enforced separation, was that he had a lot more time to think about Deborah, and this must have been a factor in his growing love for her. Over all the years Monty and Deborah had been living their separate lives, those lives had been so full of other things and other people that, in simple terms, they didn't have the time to dwell on each other. Now, though, with Julia sick in Woking and Dovid living a life incompatible, shall we say, with his wife, the scene was set at least for the pair to get a lot closer, if not physically then emotionally.

What happened next was that Monty had one of his impulsive moments and responded to his heart instead of his head. There's nothing wrong with that sometimes, but if you are a senior officer involved in issues of national security, it might be an indulgence that has consequences. And it did. He set up a meeting with Israel Defence Industries and flew to Tel Aviv. There would not normally have been a problem with that. He could go there whenever he wanted. It was just unfortunate that his timing turned out to be bad.

No sooner had Monty landed at Ben Gurion Airport than in Washington the Bignall Affair blew up. You might remember, it was Lorne Bignall, who worked in Defense Procurement at the Pentagon; he was accused of being involved in industrial espionage for a French armaments company. His guilt was apparently inescapable, and there was a serious diplomatic incident between France and the US. This put a number of foreign officials working at the Pentagon under suspicion and someone dug out a file on Monty and that got passed to London and someone else asked where he was. Given that he already had a serious matter of a relationship with an Israeli national on his file, alarm bells started to ring in Whitehall, and as a consequence Monty was under surveillance during his trip.

Because of what happened on his return, his memoirs are sketchy about what happened between him and Deborah. I believe he did telephone her before setting out so she was expecting him. I don't for a moment think they did anything they could be reproached for, but from their subsequent letters they clearly had some serious discussions and I would say from that point onwards their relationship was firmly on the path to its eventual conclusion. There were certainly frustrations ahead for both of them, but I would say Monty's impulsiveness turned out to be a good thing, at least for him and Deborah, if not for his career.

What happened on his arrival back in London was that he was called in to an interview with the Ministry's internal security department. This itself was a revelation, because as he sat on the opposite side of a large desk from a youngish man in a very smart business suit who introduced himself, with all due deference, at this stage, as Major Cowdray, he saw something of the utmost interest. The Major put a file down on the desk and in the half second it took to open it Monty read on the cover the words 'Mr Wilson'. Even upside down there was no mistaking it. His file, for some reason he could not begin to fathom, said Mr Wilson on it. Why? Who was Mr Wilson and what on Earth did he have to do with Monty? His brain wasn't so addled by what had happened in Jerusalem that he could not now shift immediately into professional mode. He tried to compute every possibility, but he had never even known anyone with that name, if he discounted the former Prime Minister, Harold Wilson, and even in the byzantine world of the security services the chance of him being concerned with Monty was nil. He had been in office when Monty was in Northern Ireland, and certainly more than one of Monty's reports, even as a captain, would have filtered through to the PM's desk. But he decided the connection was so extremely tenuous it could be disregarded. Anyway, the very way it was printed - 'Mr Wilson' - struck Monty as odd. Why would his file have someone else's name on it?

He couldn't answer any of these questions and in any case there wasn't time, because Cowdray wanted to ask a lot of questions himself, and he was impatient for answers. Monty decided to come clean and admit he had seen Deborah. He assumed they would know that and he didn't want to get caught out lying. He played it down though. She was an old friend from when he had served in Africa, he was sure they had that information. He had valid business in Israel and presented his interrogator with a brief report on his meetings with IDI officials, all of which would go on the record. The Major wanted to know if the woman he met was married and Monty was able to reply truthfully not only that she was but that on his previous visit he had had dinner with her and her husband. He went on to include Deborah's brother in this dinner party and at Avrom's name he detected a slight change in the other man's demeanour. Why did Avrom mean anything to an internal security department in Whitehall?

Monty answered all the questions he was asked but he couldn't answer the ones that kept spinning round in his head. He left the interview with nothing more than a note in his file that there might be something going on but they couldn't find it. It was better than it might have been. But he didn't leave with any answers himself. In fact, he had more questions now than before. He needed to find out who Mr Wilson was.

It was more than another twenty four hours before his brain finished computing what had happened, and it was as he was sitting eating his dinner in the flat the following evening that the penny dropped. He put his knife and fork down and wondered why he hadn't seen it. Avrom. This is underlined in his memoirs. Suddenly, it all revolved around Deborah's brother. In his mind these were different worlds - his work in one and Deborah in the other. But of course they weren't different at all. Avrom worked for the Mossad. He appeared everywhere Monty was - in Washington and London, and there he was back in his own country when Monty visited. It started to come back to him, how Avrom had appeared out of nowhere at Ben Gurion Airport. And he saw in his mind's eye Avrom flashing some kind of identity card at the IDI official, and how that changed everything. And Mr Wilson, why did Deborah know about him? In one of her letters she made a comment, and at the office the next day he searched through the pile to find it. There it was, 'I did ask Avi, but he said I shouldn't concern myself and he seemed a bit worried that I was asking. I don't know what it's about or who he is, but the feeling I get is that unless it's a problem for you you would be best to forget about him'.

How was Avrom involved with Mr Wilson, and how much did Deborah really know?

And he was frustrated that he didn't know who Mr Wilson was. He tried to think what contacts he had who might give him information, but decided that even asking was dangerous. Clearly, his file had some big question marks in it. 'They' had doubts about his loyalty. But if that were true, why didn't they reduce or even revoke his security clearance?

And most importantly, where did Deborah fit into all this? Was she using him? Was she feeding information to Israeli Intelligence through Avrom? He tried to think what he had ever told her about his work, and decided he hadn't. She had never asked. It just wasn't something either of them had had any interest in discussing. It didn't make sense. He thought further back, to the time when Avrom had encouraged him to get back in contact with Deborah. That surely was a classic ploy to set up a line of information. But if that were true, why had no-one ever actually asked him anything? He didn't carry Department papers with him, there were none at his flat, so the opportunity to spy on him was pretty well non-existent.

And in any case, what did he do in his job that might be of interest to the Mossad? He worked on covert surveillance equipment, but much of that came from Israel itself, so why would they need the little information he could provide when it was on their doorstep? He assumed that Israel Defence Industries passed information to their government, so what possible use could Monty be?

He went over and over the permutations in his head and none of them made sense. Well, he would see pretty soon if 'they' were going to take action, because they would have to reduce his security clearance, or even take him off his present job. Would they? Well, time would tell. This section of his memoirs ends with a lot of questions and no answers. At this point he decided to move Deborah's letters to the flat. Julia was unlikely to be returning in the near future and he had little doubt his office would be discreetly combed for incriminating evidence. While his letters if anything would clear him of passing information to Deborah, they were very personal and he simply didn't want Ministry snoopers reading them. Under the circumstances, he couldn't just walk out of the building with a large box in his arms, so he took a few out each evening in his briefcase. They wouldn't go as far as searching that. My guess is that they had already read the letters. It would be one explanation why they didn't take any action against him.

I was interested to see after reading this what Monty would do about Deborah. Would he write, or would he just break off their relationship? How much would their recent revelations affect his judgment? In the event he did what most people do when they can't make up their minds - he did nothing. His memoirs clearly show a great deal of indecision; he was putting off making a decision and, in fairness, what information did he have on which to base one?

And then, a few weeks later, something happened which changed everything anyway. This was the time Monty's name first appeared on the front pages of the national Press, when his picture was on every news-stand and every breakfast table, not to mention the briefing notes going to cabinet ministers, and not just in Britain. If his superiors at the Ministry had been dithering about what to do with a decorated senior officer who was giving them trouble, after this they really were in a pickle, because Monty became a hero, and the only thing you can do with heroes is decorate them again and bask in their reflected glory.

The story was told over and over again in all the papers, and Monty's own memoirs cover it in detail of course. Monty's own memory of the events does not always match the Press stories and you, like me, would undoubtedly give his version of events credence. But whoever you believe, there are certain facts that stand out, not least of which is his extraordinary bravery. Col Monty Sutherland was a man to be reckoned with.

By now it was early summer and on the morning in question Monty was in his office on the second floor at the rear of the Ministry. His window gave a panoramic view of the River Thames, and on this particular morning the river was doing its best to impress, with the early sunlight reflecting off a million ripples on the water. Anyone would have stopped and looked, and Monty was not immune to the wonder of the sight.

Then something happened. Something that you or I would not have noticed, or if we had would not have thought much of. A launch appeared from upstream and as it came opposite the Ministry building it slowed. It was that change in speed that attracted Monty's eye. His experience in anti-terrorist work had left him with an immediate suspicion of anything, even the smallest thing, that was different or unexpected. Was this unexpected? Why should a launch not slow at that place? To the uninitiated there is probably no answer, but something went off in Monty's brain. Probably it wasn't so much an alarm at this stage as simply an interest. The launch slowed and that alone kept his attention, whereas had it just continued on its path he would immediately have forgotten it.

Now he was watching it, at this stage perhaps just out of

curiosity and the launch did something that did start to ring alarm bells in his mind. It started to turn. Now the tide was quite strong that day; Monty had already noted that from the way the smaller boats were struggling to progress upstream. There was no jetty, nowhere to land, so why was the launch turning? Monty scanned the boat much more carefully now.

There was a man at the wheel and another two were in the stern, leaning on a tarpaulin that covered .... something. He couldn't tell what it was. Anyone watching would have said it was just some load they were carrying, but there was something Monty didn't like about it. He glanced down and saw the Royal Military Police sergeant at his usual place. To him this was just another boring day, guarding the rear entrance to the Ministry, a place where nothing ever happened. He was on duty but off-guard.

Monty remembered later that he had wanted to open the window and shout down some warning to the sergeant, but on reflection he felt he had no justification to do so. Had he been, say, standing with him having a chat he might have said, 'Look at that boat, does that seem suspicious to you?', but to open the window and shout would have been dramatic, and if there was nothing to it that would have even been over-dramatic. For that stupid reason the sergeant was to die.

At that moment Monty noticed that the man in the wheelhouse also had a tarpaulin, and at that moment he was removing it, as were the two men in the stern with theirs. It all happened in a flash of time, but later Monty was to write that his memory of it was in slow motion, that every tiniest action was recorded in his memory, and would be for ever.

The man at the wheel pulled back the cocking lever of a heavy machine gun at exactly the same time as the other two dropped a bomb into the mouth of a mortar. Monty didn't see anything else because he was already in the corridor. The official enquiry asked him why he didn't shout a warning to anyone to get out, but Monty knew that was useless. There were seconds only to do something and no-one gets out in seconds. They would have to take their chances. The only chance Monty had of doing anything at all was to get down there. As he flew down the staircase to the back door he heard the familiar sound of the machine gun opening up. Rounds ripped into the stone wall of the building, through the windows and beyond. They were firing a weapon with a range of more than half a mile, a gun capable of firing a thousand rounds a minute and they were shooting at close range. A weapon like that will cut a man to pieces, and by the time Monty arrived at the door the MP was a bloody mess on the ground.

Rounds were thumping into the stonework all around him as he skidded to a halt behind a pillar. He could just see the Embankment, the road between the Ministry and the river. Cars were screeching to a halt now and the air was filled with screaming. He remembered hearing that, even above the clatter of the gun. He could see the mortarmen loading a second round and at that moment it occurred to him he didn't remember hearing the first explosion. He simply assumed it had gone off but he hadn't noticed in the confusion.

Then he spotted it. The MP's submachine gun was lying in the doorway, apparently undamaged. The enquiry concluded that the weapon must have been thrown by the force of the attack across the path and into the building and because of this it was unharmed. Monty grabbed it and checked the magazine. It was fully loaded. His training now started to pay off. His actions were exactly those expected of a soldier. There was fear but no panic in his movements. He refitted the magazine and cocked the weapon. He knew there were thirty rounds, against a heavy machine gun being fed a continuous belt of heavy-calibre ammunition. The only thing in his favour was the element of surprise. No-one would be looking for him.

Luckily (if luck is an appropriate word for such a day), there were cars strewn all over the road by now. Most of the people caught in the firing line were either lying dead on the tarmac or had managed to flee. Monty leapt from one car to another and managed to reach the pavement by the river bank without being spotted. Then he emptied his magazine into the boat. He would later admit he didn't take aim at the enemy; he was calm but not that calm. His action was enough though. Several of his rounds hit the launch's fuel tank and the whole lot went up in an enormous explosion. As the huge fireball erupted, Monty was conscious of mortar rounds and machine gun ammunition exploding at the same time, but within seconds everything sank beneath the water and soon the sound of the explosions was muffled and then they died.

For just a second it all seemed terribly silent. Then the screaming started again and now the air was filled with sirens. It was only now that Monty noticed the pain in his shoulder and looking down saw blood seeping through his uniform, turning the khaki black. And then there were black-clad men, carrying what Monty recognised as Heckler and Koch submachine guns, the favoured weapon of the British security services and police. There was a nasty moment when two of them pointed their weapons at him (he still had the MP's gun in his hands) but seeing his bloodstained uniform gave him the benefit of the doubt and allowed him to get his warrant card out and identify himself. Then he fainted.

The official enquiry showed a total death toll of seven civilians in the road, three military and one civilian employee in the Ministry, and one sergeant of the Royal Military Police. There were a few wounded, but the kind of weapon used produces dead rather than wounded. The IRA claimed responsibility for the attack.

Given the ferociousness of the attack the final toll was relatively light. The most remarkable thing was that the mortar bomb, the only one they got off, failed to explode. On forensic examination it turned out to be a home-made job, and someone got it wrong. There were enough clues on it that the police were able to make a number of arrests. (In the event those arrested served only a few years and were then released as part of the agreement made by the British government in exchange for the decommissioning of IRA weapons. That, though, was a political decision and it was also rather later and doesn't concern our story.)

The wreck of the launch was recovered and on examination, whilst the mortar was home-made, the gun was a British Army General-Purpose Machine Gun, and a further investigation was started to discover how such a weapon found its way into the hands of terrorists.

The office in which the dud mortar bomb landed was on the first floor of the building and sitting at his desk at that very moment was Major Cowdray, the man who kept a file on him marked 'Mr Wilson'. The events of that summer's day changed Monty's fortunes for ever. Now, he was a national hero. He was awarded the Military Cross and he was interviewed by every newspaper from London to Washington and beyond. His picture even appeared in the Jerusalem Post, and years later Deborah's collection of his letters turned up a faded cutting.

When Monty was discharged from the King Edward VII Hospital for Officers, Rosie accompanied him to get his second medal. The MC looked particularly impressive pinned next to his sling and it made an excellent picture for the papers. And when his regiment gave a dinner in his honour, he took Rosie as his escort. Dressed in a dove-grey silk gown that set off her fresh complexion perfectly (Monty didn't know she even had such a thing, the gown that is, not the fresh complexion) she was a young lady to turn heads, and some of the younger officers round the table kept theirs turned permanently in her direction. But seeing the man of the hour engaged in sign language with this vision confused them hopelessly and not one dared approach her.

It was Rosie's first outing as a young woman and she cherished the memory of it, which she told me many years later. She was clearly quite in awe of her father, but in a nice way, a way that has no fear.

After the fuss died down, Monty left the Ministry with a problem. They had on their hands a twice-decorated national hero, but one whom they didn't quite trust, despite the fact that he had never actually done anything he shouldn't. They needed to be seen to be doing something worthwhile with him, but what use does a nation have for a hero in peacetime? They had another problem; the IRA has a long memory and they wanted to get Monty away at least from the British Isles where he was at the greatest risk.

Their salvation came from an unexpected quarter. As I said, Monty's fame spread far and wide, and the Secretary of State for Defence was asked to see the Prime Minister, who had received a letter from the Secretary General of the United Nations asking that Col Sutherland be re-assigned to him as an advisor at the highest level. The Defence Secretary didn't need asking twice. At a stroke, Monty was off their hands in a place where he couldn't possibly get into any trouble. There was further publicity about the posting, which the Ministry placed to ensure the IRA knew he would be out of the country. If he was going to get bumped off, better for everyone if it happened far away.

And for good measure, commensurate with such a high-level posting, they promoted him to Brigadier.

Monty took Julia with him to New York. She was well enough to travel and she longed to be in America again.

There, her family would see more of her and Monty was not unhappy about that. Wladek Kurtanjek, Julia's father, had a heart attack and died the week after they arrived in New York. Julia took a turn for the worse and was unable to attend the funeral, but Monty went.

Despite the seriousness of the occasion, there were people at the funeral who recognised Monty from the papers, even out of uniform, and he was a bit of a celebrity. The guests included a number of business men and Monty had more than one invitation to visit to 'talk about the 'opportunities' in the US armaments industry. Monty had long ago decided he didn't want to work in the US armaments industry and I think he was also a little flattered by all the fuss and his new job, not to mention his promotion, and by now he must have been happy to look at the Army as a job for life. By this time he was 47, and if he was going to make a break this would have been the opportunity, before it was too late to start a new career. But he didn't. The Army had been good to him, given him a home and a purpose. He would be loyal to it until he retired. Some might say that is the easy way out, that it shows a lack of adventure. I'm not going to defend Monty; he was what he was. All I would say is, what's wrong with that? I think the Army had given Monty more adventure than the average man is ever likely to see and, come to that, working for an arms company sounds glamorous but Monty already had a glamorous job.

Actually, his new posting to the UN was at such a high level that he was now little more than a figurehead, and he was disappointed to find it rather boring. He had for a while regretted no longer being a fighting man and the unexpected action he saw in London had whetted his appetite for a spot of real soldiering. It was after all the fuss had died down and he was settling into the relatively dull routine in New York that Deborah is mentioned again in his memoirs. I don't say he had forgotten her these past weeks, but this was the first time he had said anything in writing. Actually, he didn't say anything really; he simply wrote her name. He did that several times over a period of several weeks, sometimes just the name, sometimes followed by a question mark. Plainly she was on his mind, but equally I don't believe he knew what to think. The recent events and all the upheaval of moving to the States had been a good opportunity to duck the issue of where he stood with Deborah, and what to do about Avrom and whatever mischief he was up to.

The comments in his memoirs became more frequent and more elaborate, and one can see that he was using them to explore his feelings. It must have been agonising. There was so much at stake; his career and all that had happened so suddenly, but his love for Deborah as well, because I don't see that he ever stopped loving her. After their last exchange of letters I suspect he had passed some sort of watershed. He knew that, come what may, even if it took a very long time, he was going to be with her. He couldn't see how, given the fact that they were both married, but I'm sure something happened after those letters and that he was now set on that course. If I learned one thing about Monty Sutherland, it was that when he set his mind on something it was likely to happen.

Can anyone decide what is going to happen if they can't see their way through to it? Is it just pie in the sky to say, I'm going there or, I will have such and such? Well, the proof of the pudding is in the eating.

In the end Monty did something really quite unexpected, by which I mean a bit canny and therefore not in character. (I say that without the benefit of having met him, so I may have misjudged him in that way, but I always think of him as a very straightforward person, not a canny one). In fact what he did was hardly cunning really - he wrote to Avrom.

New York
3rd September 1991

Dear Avrom

As you will see, I am back in New York. There was a spot of trouble in London, well, not trouble really, you might have read about it. I've been posted to the UN as special adviser to the Secretary General, which is a lot less exciting than it sounds.

Anyway, I just thought I would drop you a line to let you know. Do write and let me know what you are up to. I trust the family are all well.

Best wishes
Monty Sutherland

It was hardly forthcoming. What did he hope to gain from such a brief note? Well, I guess he was opening doors. If he had no way to find out what Avrom was up to, and whether Deborah was part of it, he needed at least to re-establish contact. It was the only chance he had of finding out. Had he just left it, who knows if that would have been the end of his relationship with Deborah?

Was he expecting a reply from Avrom? Or would he just magically turn up, like he always did? He faxed a letter to Monty's office.

Netanya
October 5, 1991

Dear Monty

By now you will be wanting some explanations. It's time we talked. I can fly over on Friday and be in New York in the evening. Perhaps you would reserve a table for us at the usual restaurant?

Yours

Avrom Mandelstam

Monty's note on receiving this fax, a note even more terse than his own, is itself brief, but it gives some idea of how he felt. There was a question first - why hadn't Avrom telephoned, given the urgency of the meeting? He guessed the answer to that was that someone who doesn't want to be asked any questions doesn't pick up the phone. He wanted to be facing Monty when he explained.

And clearly he did want to explain. Was he really flying over to New York specially to talk with Monty? Even Monty's own expense account (and he was a brigadier) didn't run to a transatlantic flight to have dinner, so this was important - to Avrom, to the Mossad, perhaps to Israel. Monty was important. In that he had been right. The Mossad needed him. But that didn't tell him how Deborah was involved, or indeed if she was involved.

His next thought was that meeting Avrom itself could be dangerous. But Avrom had thought of that; now he thought about himself he saw the sense of meeting at the restaurant. If they were going to be followed, far better a meeting in a public place than at Monty's apartment. And if British Intelligence were in on this, they would surely know the moment Avrom went through immigration control at JFK. Monty didn't know much about these things but he assumed Avrom's Israeli passport would set computers talking across the ether and some duty officer somewhere in New York would take a printout to his senior officer and he in turn would tell someone in London who would connect the arrival with Monty and arrange immediately for a tail. Or was he being paranoid? He imagined that right now, in some office in the far reaches of MI6, Mr Wilson was peering intently at some computer screen and plotting his next move. I think at this point Monty was getting a little paranoid because, in my experience, MI6 are not that good. They tend to know about these things afterwards rather than before.

The restaurant Avrom had asked Monty to book was a Jewish one on the East Side. They had gone there several times over the years; Monty liked the food more than he had expected and Avrom obviously felt comfortable there. When Monty arrived, instead of one of the usual tables he was taken by the head waiter through the main restaurant and shown to a private dining room at the back. Avrom was already there. Monty knew at once that this restaurant was Mossad territory.

They spent a pleasant evening eating good food and talking about nothing in particular. Monty was wary but Avrom had a way of putting him at his ease. By the end of the evening Monty didn't remember having discussed any of the matters that were on his mind, and yet he came away feeling reassured. Certainly Avrom said something to the effect that Monty could trust him, that they were on the same side, and even that Deborah was not using him, and all without saying it in as many words. In practical terms, Avrom asked him to wait for a couple of days and then all would be revealed. That night as he prepared for bed, Monty shook his head and tried to understand what it had all been about. But he wanted to trust Avrom, because he wanted to trust Deborah, and he let that desire sway him. In the event, his instinct was proved right.

Two days later Monty got a request from the Secretary General of the UN to meet him the following day. No files or notes would be needed. When he walked into his boss's office he got one of the biggest shocks of his life. There were two other men sitting around the conference table, and one of them was Avrom Mandelstam. Monty stood there, unable to compute this, but the DG got up and with his usual smile welcomed Monty and offered him a chair. He introduced the other man as the Director of the International Atomic Energy Agency.

A secretary poured Monty a cup of coffee and slipped

out of the room. He heard the door close with a loud click that seemed to say this meeting was confidential. The DG let him pour milk into his coffee and stir it. Monty tried to use these seconds to think, but he had nothing to base a judgment on. It just didn't compute, and he decided to stop thinking and listen.

The Secretary General explained that the IAEA was an affiliated organisation of the UN, and that it had the job of monitoring the acquisition of nuclear materials by countries that had signed the nuclear non-proliferation treaty. Monty was vaguely aware of this but that was all. He went on to explain that for some time there had been intelligence coming in that nuclear materials were being supplied to Syria, a country that the UN was very concerned about in terms of nuclear capability. At this stage they still didn't know whether the materials were being acquired by the government or if this was an unofficial operation, but the assumption had to be for the time being that the government of Syria was trying to build a nuclear weapon.

That, inevitably, was of the utmost concern to the Israeli government, and hence Avrom, although an officer in the Israel Defence Force, had been working undercover for the Mossad as part of the Israeli effort to cooperate with the IAEA. He had for some time been reporting both to his own government and the UN, at the highest level, which of course meant the Secretary General. Almost no-one outside this room knew of the operation. The UN did not want its concerns to get into the public arena, which would embarrass the Syrians and God only knew what it would do to the Americans. It might eventually have to come to that, with the US invading Syria or perhaps bombing nuclear installations.

The Secretary General paused to let Monty take all this in. Monty processed information quickly when he had to, and he was waiting for the rest of it. That was the next bombshell.

Syria could get nuclear materials from Russia. There were any number of senior people there who could lay their hands on the stuff for a price. But that wasn't what Avrom had been working on. To build a nuclear weapon you need certain electronic devices for detonation. There were few suppliers of such equipment. One of them was KTX industries.

Now, all three men looked at Monty. He put his coffee cup down and folded his hands together to stop them shaking and stared intently at the grain of the desktop. He didn't trust himself to say anything so there was no option but to continue listening.

The Israeli government had been cooperating fully with the UN in return for not invading Syria themselves, but time was limited. There was an agreement that an invasion would be held off to give the UN a chance to deal with the problem first. Avrom had unlimited resources at his disposal to this end, but he needed access to KTX. It hardly needed to be said that that was why Monty was there. At last, the question was asked openly; would Monty help? The DG could arrange to have his posting made semi-permanent but there was the question of divided loyalties. He wouldn't be able to talk to London about it, so in effect he would be working for two masters. Avrom knew Monty had a 'Mr Wilson' file but he didn't yet know what that meant; it was assumed it had something to do with his relationship with Deborah (Monty cast his eyes down to the desk again at this but no-one commented. They knew about it). He would need some time to think about it and the DG gave another of his big smiles that said the meeting was over.

The DG made the slightest sign that Avrom should accompany Monty, and the two left the room together. They walked silently to the canteen and sat down to another coffee which Monty didn't want but he needed to do something. Naturally they couldn't say anything, but Avrom brought up the subject of Deborah. Monty shouldn't worry - he had known for a long time, and he also knew that Deborah had not been unfaithful to her husband, at least not what he would call unfaithful, so he had no problem with the relationship. Coming from a younger man Monty wasn't sure how to take that, but he wasn't sure about a lot of things and that was just another.

The upshot of the conversation was that Monty could be quite sure Deborah had not been working with Avrom. In fact she knew nothing about his work (and mustn't either). If Monty agreed to the assignment he would be able to tell her nothing. On the other hand at least, Avrom hoped, they would be able to get back in touch with each other. It was like he was giving Monty his approval to have an affair with his sister. Monty looked Avrom squarely in the eye for a moment to judge the man, and then said he had already decided to accept the job.

New York
13th October 1991

Dear Deborah

It has been a long time since I wrote last, and I am quite sure you have been worrying about things. I know you rang once and I am truly sorry I didn't return your call. You know I have in the past been on assignments that have had to be secret. Well, this is the reason for my silence. I hope you'll understand it was unavoidable. I have wanted to say so much to you, and I hope you won't mind if I say those things now, after all these months.

You must know that I love you. I always have. I know I shouldn't. There is Julia, and her illness is no excuse, but I loved you before I ever met her. And what about Dovid? Is he having an affair? I suppose it's important to me because, to put it bluntly, it would give me moral justification, although I would still love you regardless. I guess moral justification would be a good thing to have right now though.

You said you want me. I hope you remember saying that, because I am going to hold you to it. Not now, but one day. I shall for the foreseeable future be involved in difficult situations with my work, but I promise you that does not involve physical danger. For now, I am based in New York, with the United Nations. I expect you read in your papers about my little excitement in London. Well, they've shipped me out here to keep me out of harm's way, and Julia has come with me so, although she is staying in Washington I do see her frequently.

The other news is that her father died. I can't say I shall miss him. His son, Victor, approached me at the funeral and wanted me to join KTX, like his father had. I said I would think about it. This job is frankly getting on my nerves and after the way the Army treated me back in London I might just do it. They gave me another gong (you remember my gong, don't you?) and promoted me, so I'm a Brigadier now, which looks most impressive in parade uniform but is otherwise nothing special.

Rosie has been out to have a look at the university. Do you remember me telling you about it? I went with her and I must say I was impressed. I think she'll decide to go and I'm sure she would be happy there. She takes her exams next summer and her teachers reckon she will do brilliantly. I don't think she has any firm idea about a career - obviously there are great limitations on what a deaf person can do. But she has enormous pluck and I will support whatever she wants to do. If I join KTX the extra money will help in that respect.

Deborah - do please write. Don't be angry with me for my silence. Do you trust me? I have seen Avrom here and he knows it was unavoidable so ask him. Write and tell me its OK.

All my love

Monty

[Editor's note. This was the first time I had ever heard Monty lie to Deborah. It can't have been easy for him.]

Jerusalem
October 27, 1991

Dear Monty

Of course it's OK. I know what your work means - you don't have to excuse it. You have had times like this before, although I did think you didn't do it any longer. But don't worry, you don't have to explain anything to me. I trust you completely.

As it happens Avi has been in New York recently and he rang from Netanya to say he had met you. Apparently you like Jewish food! That's good. One day I will cook for you and you will know what Jewish food really tastes like - not like that stuff they serve in America.

OK, I admit I was worried, but worried for you, not about you, if you know what I mean. I read in the papers about your heroic exploit in London and naturally I panicked, but then I thought you must be alright because they said you were, and if you were dead I was sure they would have said so. Avi said your shoulder was hit but that you're better now. You might like to know I am a specialist in gunshot wounds so if, God forbid, it ever happens again, just call me and I'll fly over immediately! Seriously - you're too old to be getting shot at, so just stop it, will you? I don't want to lose you now - not now I know you love me.

Which means I'm allowed to tell you that I love you. No, it doesn't really, because I'm married and you're married and we're not supposed to love anyone else, but I'm afraid life is too short to worry about all of that. I don't know what the future will be for us, or if there is a future at all, but there is a present and I am no longer going to deny it. Actually, we have a past too, don't we? It's longer than most married couples.

So from now on you must tell me everything (well, not absolutely everything, I mean about your work, I don't need to know about that), but everything else. I want to know about your life, about Rosie, even perhaps about Julia. I need to be part of your life, and that can only be if you tell me about it. I can't imagine any of it. What your home is like, or your office, or what you eat for breakfast (no, don't send me a menu, please). But do send me photographs. I need to see your life. That way I can feel closer to you.

Well, I'm going on like a schoolgirl, and I'm a grown woman. You make me feel younger, and that's not a bad thing is it? I wonder when I will see you?

All my love

Deborah

New York
11th November 1991

Dear Deborah

Your letter was wonderful. And it was a relief that you understand. I'm sending you some photographs so you can see what my life looks like in pictures. The one of Rosie was taken in the Mess at the dinner the regiment gave me. She's lovely, isn't she? Some of the younger men were going gooey just looking her but drooling is not attractive in an officer. Anyway, they were confused by her deafness, so she was left in peace. Actually, I do hope that's not going to be an obstacle for her. Young men don't find it easy (I know) and that kind of barrier is obviously going to be a problem. Still, I think she will overcome it - it's just that she has had so little to do with young men she doesn't know what to do herself. I daresay she will be chatting them up somehow once she gets the hang of it. She's only eighteen.

Well, now she's over here ready to start at Gallaudet, the university I've been telling you about. She going to be doing a mathematics degree - she's always loved maths. I can't tell you how proud I am of her. Julia wanted her to stay with her family, which I can understand, but she very much wanted to stay on campus, which I can also understand. She's starting a whole new part of her life, in a foreign country, so it's important she has the opportunity to live and socialise with her peer group.

Julia has her ups and downs. She has had to stop driving, which is a blow for her, because now she's dependent on other people. The Kurtanjeks are wealthy so it's not a problem, but for her personally being driven is not the same. She can be a little unsteady on her legs sometimes, so now she has a full-time companion, a very nice lady called Marcia, and I think she sees her as a friend as much as a nursemaid, which helps.

I go down to see her most weekends but her brother, Victor, always seems to be around and he's getting on my nerves a bit. He never misses an opportunity to talk about KTX and he can't understand why I'm not jumping at the chance to work for them. Actually, if it weren't for him I would be interested. It would depend how independent I would be, with him as President now. I'm still thinking it over. Frankly I can't understand why he thinks I would be such an asset. My Army rank seems to mean more to him than it does to me. And I do have an awful lot of contacts throughout NATO, so I guess it's not that difficult to understand. And with Julia here now, it might be better to stay in the States permanently instead of going back to the UK after this posting if she can't come with me. It depends on how her illness progresses I suppose.

Well, I don't have to decide right now. To be honest, my more immediate concern is how I can get to see you. Any ideas?

With love

Monty

Jerusalem
November 23, 1991

Dear Monty

Good news! I've been invited to a WHO conference in New York. OK, I got myself invited. They pay all my expenses, so I'll have three days in a nice hotel in return for sitting listening to other people giving papers for a change. Actually, it will also give me a chance to meet some sponsors for our African medical students (you remember of course, Issy's scheme?).

It's not until next month, but since I see you about once every ten years I guess we can wait another few weeks.

I'll telephone you with the details.

Love

Deborah

Monty's memoirs show a marked change at this point. He sounds like an excited schoolboy. And his disappointment was therefore all the worse when Deborah rang to say she couldn't make the trip because her daughter had had an accident. It was nothing serious - a broken leg - but she just couldn't go off the day after it happened. Monty, as ever, put a brave face on it when he spoke with Deborah, but in his notes he hides his feelings less successfully.

It's not hard to imagine their frustration. Your children come before all else, and I think Deborah had a lot of guilt about the hours she worked anyway and, given that she wasn't actually speaking at the conference, there really was no option but to cancel. When I read about it I pictured Monty stuck in New York and Deborah in Israel, and it came to me that their relationship really was terribly fragile. How do you sustain love over such a long time, and such great distances? Does it signify a greater type of love, something special? Or is it merely an obsession? In that situation, would you stop sometimes and wonder, if you actually did get together, whether it would work, or whether it only worked because you weren't together? Loving someone is not the same as living with them.

So was it a romance that should never be put to the ultimate test? Of course, as Monty's biographer, I know the answer to that question, but the reader will forgive me (I hope) if I keep that secret a little longer.

In the event it wasn't long before the pair did get a chance to see each other. It was in Geneva, only a few weeks later. In fact, now that they both had United Nations connections, there would be the occasional opportunity in future. I've said it before and I think its worth repeating, there is no sign that when they did meet their was anything sexual between them. I know some people will find that hard to believe, perhaps they will say I'm being naive, but

I'm reading not only what Monty says in his memoirs (and why would he hide it?) but also what he doesn't say, and I can find nothing.

No, I really do see their love as platonic. Well, perhaps platonic is not quite the right word, because I believe that suggests it was deliberately non-physical. I would say their relationship excluded sex because it had to. I know, millions of couples don't let such matters as being married to someone else worry them, but perhaps that was one thing Monty and Deborah had in common - respect. They did respect their spouses, if not enough to end their relationship then enough not to do anything that would conform to the world's judgment of unfaithfulness. Perhaps they felt that gave them the moral high ground, enough anyway to justify their love. That what they didn't do meant it was alright to do what they did do. I don't know, of course.

Another matter on which I can only speculate is whether at this time Deborah's husband, Dovid, was himself really having an affair. If he was would that have given Deborah justification? Most women would have said so, but perhaps she was responding to what Monty felt, and his wife was not only not being unfaithful but she had a very serious illness. Anyone would feel pretty guilty cheating on a wife that sick. And anyway, why can't two people love each other without jumping into bed?

New York
15th December 1991

My Dear Deborah

What can I say without sounding like I blame you? When I say that I completely understand about Yael, I trust you to believe I am being sincere

You said I sounded angry on the phone. No, I'm not angry. Well, OK, I am angry, but not at you, just at the situation, a situation that's not of your making. Do you think I should be angry with you, that I should be more demanding - want more? That would be childish. It would be putting on you the responsibility for our situation. You are no more responsible than I am. I'm as married as you, if not more (I mean given your husband's situation) so I am at least half the problem.

You say I am too reasonable, so English. I am, I admit, a realist. I don't ask for what I can't have. And right now, I can't have you.

With all my love

Monty

PS. Don't write back immediately. The office will be closed over Christmas and I don't want a letter from you lying around (with an Israeli stamp), waiting for someone to take an interest in it.

Jerusalem
January 7, 1992

Dear Monty

Happy new year (no, we don't celebrate it, but you do). Another year gone. Wasted. You say you don't want what you can't have. Well, maybe if you wanted it more you would find you could have it. Life is too short to be waiting for ever until you can have.

Love

Deborah

New York
21st January 1992

Dear Deborah

I'm not waiting. If you say that it sounds like I'm waiting for Julia to die, and I couldn't think such a thing. I hate to say this, but as long as she is sick I will be tied to her. And she will be sick until she dies. And that means, like it or not, that I am waiting for her to die. It's true. I can't escape the facts.

Waiting is one thing, though, wanting is another. I don't want Julia to die. It's not within me to want such a thing, even though it would give me my freedom. So I won't allow myself even to think such a thing.

I can't have you until the thing I don't want to happen does happen, and I want you, so does a part of me really want it to happen? Am I living a lie?

When I sit with her and we talk, I try to analyse what I feel. Do I still love her, or is it just pity (or even guilt)? I tell myself she needs me, but even that isn't really true. She has her family and her companion, Marcie. I almost feel like an intruder when I go down at the weekend. We can't go out much, maybe for a drive in the country so she had a change of scenery, but not to the theatre or dinner or anything. Friends have stopped inviting us for dinner. I think they find illness embarrassing, and if we do see anyone they overcompensate by making too much of a *fuss of her. Then when I get back to New York colleagues ask after her health solicitously, but they don't know her and why would they even be interested? They're supposed to ask so they do, and I'm supposed to tell them and I do, but no-one actually means any of it, so you could say we're all living a lie.*

I'm sorry, I didn't mean to go on like this. Perhaps I shouldn't send you this.

Love

Monty

Jerusalem
February 15, 1992

Dearest Monty

I got back from the airport and all I could think about was you. Don't blush but I could still taste your lips. Anyway, when I got in to the apartment Dovid was there. I must have gone bright red myself, because the way he was looking at me it looked like he knew.

But it wasn't that. He must have spent the whole three days planning what he was going to say to me, and it all came out. He has been seeing someone else - a journalist at the magazine where he works. I've been asking myself why he told me, but then I found out a mutual friend knows, and the two of them have had a big row, so I guess Dovid thought this man would tell me to get back at him. As it happens he didn't, so maybe he is a better friend than Dovid thinks, but in any case he told me for nothing but he can't take it back and now I know, and he knows I know, so we can't pretend any longer.

So we had a big fight and he said he would move out but he hasn't but he has moved into the spare bedroom, which can't be very comfortable because we use it as a store not a bedroom so he's sleeping in a cupboard really. Still, that's his problem. I've told him he can go any time he likes. I earn a lot more than him so I don't need him financially now, and Yael is 10 and very independent, so I don't think she would even notice if her father didn't live here, what with the strange hours he works anyway.

So I'm afraid, my darling, that my dream of you was shattered and has stayed shattered because with so much to think about you will understand I need to decide what it is I feel about my husband before I think about you and me. I do wonder though why we insist on being so puritanical (is that what you would say?). Well, for me anyway. Of course, you have your wife to think about.

What I can tell you, because I don't need to think about it, is that I love you.

Love

Deborah

While all this emotional upheaval was going on, Monty was in the throes of becoming involved with what he called Operation Swordfish (it was a code word he made up. It must have been his Army background, or the schoolboy in him, because no-one else called it anything at all).

The first part of the deception was to join KTX Industries without resigning his commission in the Army. Neither KTX not the Army could know he was working for both. One unexpected result of this deception was that he was suddenly being paid two salaries. His income as a Brigadier was not insubstantial, and it was supplemented by an overseas posting allowance. And the salary KTX was paying him was three times as much, so he found himself with an embarrassment of riches. He couldn't pay his KTX salary into his London bank account, so he opened a dollar account with the First Bank of Boston in the name Mr Monty Sutherland. And he never spent a cent of it. He had planned eventually to give it all back to KTX, but the way things turned out that was impossible and the money got put to rather better use. He gave the whole lot away. Half of it went to Gallaudet University to provide a bursary for poorer students, the other half eventually went to the Dr Issy Bar-On Foundation, to fund the training of African doctors at the Hadassah Hospital in Jerusalem.

As far as his time went, that was spent entirely on KTX business. There was a period of induction. When Monty did anything, he did it thoroughly. He says in his memoirs he found it easier than he expected to make the transfer from army officer to vice-president, but that because he knew he was an officer still, it was like a game to him. He threw himself into it and Victor Kurtanjek was surprised at the stamina Monty had for learning, even at his age.

Julia was delighted he was in the family business now, and her health even took a turn for the better. He does say he felt bad about deceiving her, but not as bad as he did about lying to Deborah who, remember, knew nothing about 'Operation Swordfish'. In at least one of his letters he had hinted to her that he might after all join KTX but he seems to have changed his mind and told her nothing. Was that for security reasons, or did he feel a small lie was better than a big one? Knowing Monty, I think the latter.

Avrom had no difficulty lying to his sister, but then he lied for a living.

Monty had no previous experience in this kind of work, and before he could do anything useful with Avrom a myriad of small details had to be dealt with. For example his office at the UN had to be maintained, so that if anyone called from London they would simply be told he was unavailable at that moment. Then his secretary would call him so he could call the Ministry back. But even his secretary couldn't know what he was doing because the risk of a slip up was just too great, so she was told he would be working away for a while on a hush-hush mission to ensure her loyalty. Actually, Monty made a brief comment on her - he seems to have thought she had a bit of a crush on him, and given Monty's unassuming nature I imagine it was true.

Avrom acted as postman for Monty. He collected his mail from the UN building and delivered it to him regularly when they met in Washington. Some of this was official Ministry of Defence matters but of course there were letters from and to Israel, and at this point Avrom could only have been completely au fait with Monty and his sister's correspondence. There was nothing the former could do to hide this, so he obviously didn't try.

Monty thought about the string of lies that was being told and decided it was eventually bound to collapse. Each time you put another link in the chain you increase the possibility of a mistake. That's probably in the training manual for the secret services but one has to remember that the UN wasn't a secret service and this operation had been put together very unofficially. Fortunately Avrom was in charge and he was an experienced operative.

So Monty took up his post at KTX Industries and the reports I have read suggest just about everyone there fell for his charms. He found his approach to giving orders in the modern Army worked well in business too. He was more authoritative than the average businessman, without being aggressive. And his measured British accent seemed to command extra respect.

By nature a courteous man, people did his bidding without having to be asked twice. He made a note at this time that this might in fact be his true métier, and that he could probably, if he put his mind to it, overtake Victor Kurtanjek. He was clearly in his element and enjoying the game.

But it wasn't a game at all. He knew that and he knew he would have to get down to some serious work. Not work for KTX - for the UN. His liaison with Avrom was difficult. They couldn't meet at the UN building, because as far as Victor was concerned he had no further business there. And they couldn't meet at his apartment, or at Avrom's either, because they knew that whoever Mr Wilson was he might have surveillance on these and he was likely to notice regular meetings with an Israeli known to be working for the Mossad. So they met in the back room of the Jewish restaurant in the Lower East Side.

At first all Monty could report was that he was getting to find his way round the KTX building and people were getting used to him. It was fortunate he was such a likeable person; staff there were soon telling him all sorts of things, most of which he had no interest in but which got him a reputation as someone you could talk to. One of the things they said was not to trust Victor Kurtanjek. They didn't say it in as many words, but they said it all the same.

And another of the things they said was that there was

New York
20th April 1992

Dear Deborah

Did you say Kapuchinski? That rings a bell. Yes, now I come to think of it, I do love someone called Deborah Kapuchinski. Would that be you?

Yours (for ever)

Brigadier Montgomery Sutherland

Jerusalem
April 30, 1992

Dear Monty

Why does my name ring a bell? Is that one of your quaint English expressions I haven't learned, like gongs? Bells and gongs, mmm. Or now you live in the USA, is it American? Are you picking up vulgar slang?

So you say you love me? Prove it.

Deborah

New York
9th May 1992

My dearest Deborah

In the enclosed, unmarked, sealed envelope, there is a kiss from me. Do not open it, or it will escape, but keep it safe, somewhere about your person.

Does this prove I am madly in love with you, or simply that I am mad?

Love

Monty

Jerusalem
May 21, 1992

Dear Monty

So under that uniform covered with gold braid and gongs, there beats a romantic heart. Either that or you are, as you suggest, mad. I like to believe the first.

I shall treasure your kiss - until you can give me the real thing.

With all of my love

Deborah

Agents in the field have to have enormous stamina. They have to be able to work alone for long periods, and if necessary live a double life, remembering who they have told which lie to. Monty was a pretty straight sort, and Avrom knew he wouldn't be able to keep this up for long. It was important that Monty got into the parts of KTX he hadn't yet been privy to.

But nothing goes according to plan, for those of us who live mundane lives, so I imagine those engaged in this kind of work have to constantly update their plans to absorb those things they could not have foreseen.

What both Monty and Avrom did foresee was that he might get called to London, but it happened sooner than they would have liked. He had to answer the summons and he duly presented himself at the Ministry of Defence in Whitehall. His most telling comment in his memoirs at this time was how strange it felt to be back in his old world, how it brought home the nature of his very peculiar existence. He started then to learn one of the tricks of his new trade - acting.

It was only natural that his first thought on receiving the order was that someone was on to him. Again, that's to be expected in an amateur. When he sat in the oak-panelled office at the Ministry he had a feeling of deja vu; it felt like he was about to be interrogated. But he wasn't; he was over-reacting. He was required to go back to Northern Ireland. A very old contact of his, an informant, had recently been released from prison, and was asking to speak to him. He wouldn't say what it was about but just that he had learned something important and he would only tell Monty. The Ministry was concerned to get this information, whatever it was, because the man had been reliable before and they felt it had to be something big. At the same time, they feared a trap. Many years had passed, but the IRA have long memories. Had the informant turned? Was this some plot to get revenge?

Whilst the officer briefing him didn't divulge his concerns to Monty, the latter was only too aware of the possibilities. What choice did he have? Well, he was given that choice - he could volunteer to go, or he could get on the next plane back to New York. Monty knew he shouldn't do anything to jeopardise his mission in America, but he also knew he was being watched by his masters. It was important to establish his loyalty and commitment. He was a twice-decorated officer. He couldn't refuse. To have done so would have raised doubts that could even result in his permanent recall to Britain. No, he would have to go.

It wasn't a trap. The informant did genuinely have something and Monty completed a successful mission. The only snag was the length of time it took, what with travelling, making contact (and all the subterfuge that went with that), and returning to London to brief his minders and then the Northern Ireland Minister. It was almost two weeks before he was ready to fly back to the States, and he sent a fax to Victor at KTX to say his family business there was done and he was on his way. He was also able to report, truthfully, that he had made some useful contacts while he was in London at the British Ministry of Defence. He thought that was a nice touch.

New York
24th June 1992

My Dearest Deborah

What excuse do I have this time? As if I need one! You know (I hope) I would write every day if I could. No, that's not true - I would phone every day. Or even better, I would see you every day. As it is, you didn't get a letter even.

I'm afraid I've been back on the other side of the Atlantic, my side, on a secret mission! It's all far too hush hush to tell you anything about it at all, so you will have to be content that your - your whatever I am to you, has been away on a matter of national security. Or something like that.

The good news is that no-one shot at me for a change. The worst that happened was that I banged my ankle on one of those trolleys at the airport. You may laugh, but actually it hurt like hell. Obviously I'm getting too old for dangerous missions like capturing airport trolleys.

So here I am, safely back in God's own country, and the world is a safe place again. Actually, that's not true is it? I sit over here where everyone thinks they're in some impregnable fortress, and you live in a war zone. Don't think I have forgotten that. People here and in Britain think that because Iraq was such a pushover we can take on anyone anywhere and win. I suspect they are going to get a shock one day, and I think it's going to come from your part of the world. I've lived through the cold war, when we all thought the threat was Communism, and once that went away we supposed there were no more threats.

The Middle East is going to explode one day. Most people in America are completely ignorant of history, even people at quite a high level in the military. The threat is Islam, and the Moslems have hundreds of years of defeat at the hands of the west they are one day going to avenge. I don't know when or how, but I am convinced it's coming.

This isn't the place for a history lesson, and you probably think I'm a boring old fool, but Islam's biggest enemy has always been Britain, going back to the Crusades, and finishing after the First World War when Britain and France carved the region up between themselves. I hardly have to remind you, I've served in Jordan. At that time, all the talk was about Israel, about pushing every last Jew into the sea. But Israel is just an excuse. It's not the real reason for Arab or Moslem anger.

My other fear is that if the US keeps going in this same direction, trying to be the world's policeman, it's going to put itself in the line of fire. They think here they have overwhelming military superiority but they should have learned how little that means in Vietnam. I shouldn't say this but the UN is a waste of space. It's dominated by regional interests, and if you think how many Moslem countries there are in the world, actually the Islamic vote can overwhelm even the Security Council when it comes to UN Resolutions.

I'm sorry, I didn't intend to lecture. My recent work has made me more thoughtful than I was, so please excuse me if I let off some steam. I'll *write again soon in a completely different vein.*

Love

Monty

Jerusalem
July 13, 1992

Dearest Monty

I'm very pleased no-one has been shooting at you, but it seems bullets aren't the only thing that can hurt a soldier. I would say you have lost some of your old self-confidence, and that something has happened (or is still happening) to do that to you.

I think you need a holiday. Have you thought about that? Could your wife go away with you? I expect she needs your support now. I think your work has got too much for you lately and looking after someone else would do you good. What about Rosie - you haven't written recently about her. Is her course going well? She must have finished her first year by now, so do write and tell me all the news, not about what's going on in the world.

It's Yael's birthday next week. We've agreed (I mean Dovid and me) that we'll put a brave face on it and make a party for her. I don't know how to explain our situation here, in a way you would understand. Dovid still sleeps in the other room but we're still living together, whatever that means. A friend of mine used to call it living together apart, if that makes any more sense. You can't be angry with someone all of the time, so we get along alright.

The funny thing is, he has finished with that other woman. Is that funny? Well, you know what I mean. But that doesn't mean he can just move back into my bed, so you need have no worries there. He can have as many affairs as he likes, it's nothing to do with me now. Come to that, so could I, but I don't. I'm a one-man woman, and the one man is you. What are we going to do about that?

Love

Deborah

New York
29th July 1992

My Dear Deborah

Well, I did what you said - we went on holiday, Julia, Rosie and me. Julia seemed well to start with and I was quite hopeful but she started to get very tired, and when she gets tired her speech starts to slur a little, so I know. We came back early. Still, I think it was worth going, even if Rosie was disappointed. It's a shame, because she wants to spend time with me but of course I have to look out for Julia and I can't give them both my time.

Actually, things with Julia are a bit better just now. I don't know why but she's taking more interest in me. I hope that means she's feeling better generally.

You asked about Rosie's course. It seems to going very well, as far as I can tell. She can communicate perfectly well when she wants to but when she doesn't she plays not only deaf but dumb. I'm afraid there's a boy somewhere in the story - I do hope she will be gentle with him!

Well, that's all my news for now, so I'll say good-bye.

All my love

Monty

Actually, it wasn't all his news, but it was all the news that was fit to write. The rest involved Julia.

Why did Monty's wife cover for him went he had to go to England? He wondered that while he was away. Monty's relationship with Julia is not at all clear from his memoirs, and his letters to Deborah talk of her health but not the woman herself. It would be easy to write off their marriage as one of things that seemed a good idea at the time but no-one could quite remember why. I can't speak for Julia but such a marriage is hardly what one can imagine a man like Monty going into. He might not have been the greatest when it came to picking women but he wasn't completely stupid about it either.

That Julia's illness was a tragedy for her hardly needs to be stated, but one must add to that that it did come at a bad time for her marriage. Between that and Monty's work they didn't actually spend a lot of time together. However, when they were together I suspect they were happy enough.

What does all this mean? Well, for one I think it says that Julia herself would have recognised not only the weaknesses in her marriage to Monty, but the strengths. She would have been bound to compare her husband with, say, her own family. Her father had been an unpleasant man but her brother could only be described as a nasty piece of work. I think Julia had some of the family characteristics - she could be arrogant for example, but was that something she grew up with and grew out of when she married such a kind man as Monty? I would say so.

Either way, it seems to me that she came to a point in her life when she had to make a choice between her family and her husband. It does her a great deal of credit that she chose the latter. But was it just her love for Monty that made her side with him, or was it something she really didn't like in her own family? The answer to that I can say with certainty. She knew about KTX Industry's illegal activities.

When Wladek had been President of the corporation he had treated his daughter as a kind of second-class son, which is better than it sounds because she did have some say in the running of the business she had shares in. After his death, the management style changed. There was no way Victor was going to consult his sister, or any other woman come to that.

And it was Victor who ran the operation Monty had gone in to uncover. It was his personal fiefdom. He spoke fluent Russian as well as Polish. When the Kurtanjek family had fled Warsaw in 1945 all of their property had been taken by the Soviet authorities. Victor considered himself the shield bearer for the family and he had no love of Russians. But business was business, and if selling to Russia was a bitter pill to swallow, the wealth it brought back to the family made that a lot easier.

Monty knew none of this at the time, and his primary concern was to get closer to Victor and gain his trust enough that he might learn at least something. This seemed like an impossible task, given the amount of secrecy Victor had built up around the business over the years. Why would he let Monty in on anything? Monty had nothing he could use. Until, that is, Victor hit a snag.

KTX Industries wasn't selling to the Russian Ministry of Defence, it was selling to a rather more clandestine organisation loosely connected with the security apparatus, which sourced materials not only for its own government but for foreign clients as well. Again, none of this was known yet to Monty, and I hope I'm not spoiling the story by mentioning it now, but it helps to understand why Monty was so important to Victor. Anyway, more of that later, but I can tell you Victor wasn't being as clever as he thought he was, because he misjudged Monty Sutherland. He thought everyone had a price, but that was a mistake.

Jerusalem
August 14, 1992

Dearest Monty

So now you're finding out what it's like to be the parent of a teenage daughter! That's something I have to look forward to. Yael is a precocious child and I think she will be breaking boys' hearts in not too many years from now. Does she take after her mother or her father in that respect? I'm afraid it's me. Anyway, I don't intend to break anyone's heart - you can be sure of that.

The situation with Dovid is much the same. I would never have thought two people could live like this but we do. Like friends living in the same apartment, not like a married couple. Actually that's more true than I might have realised - we are friends now. I still don't agree with his politics but we can talk, as long as the things we talk about aren't important ones. He hasn't become any less arrogant, so what is the point of telling him what I think about important issues, because he doesn't credit me with any political intelligence. He thinks because I'm a doctor and he's a journalist that I can't have an educated opinion about his world just as he doesn't know about mine. Well, he would have to study for many years to know what I know about medicine, but I read the papers here every day (not his magazine though) and I can have an opinion like anyone else.

In fact if he ever stopped to listen to me he might find we are not so different as he thinks. He went far to the left at the time I was becoming more right wing, but like a lot of people here these days I think we're both tired of the tension. It's been the same all my life, with no future we can see for our children. I think Dovid worries about the country we have created for Yael and her generation just as I do. I would be content to make peace with the Arabs now, even if we have to give up land for it. It's land we didn't want in the first place - when they attacked us we fought back and got stuck with it. Now it's become a huge issue and I wonder if we shouldn't just give it back to them and live in peace. It's only a small minority of people here - the really religious ones - who think every bit of Eretz Israel is sacred. Like the Moslems saying the Temple Mount here in Jerusalem is sacred to them. It's not - they built it on the ruins of the original Jewish Temple, which was there for hundreds of years already.

Here I am doing what you do, giving a history lesson! Sorry.

Do write more about your wife. Tell me about her symptoms, because as a doctor I can't help being interested. From the little you have said it seems her condition is deteriorating. Is that true?

Avi rang the other day from New York, and he sends his regards to you. Don't you two see each other these days?

Love

Deborah

New York
27th August 1992

Dearest Deborah

Thanks for the history lesson - seriously. You might think I'm so tied up with the affairs of nations here at the UN but I do have an interest in Israel, and actually not only because of you. I wonder if it goes back to growing up in Cyprus? You remember that day when we were there (how could you forget?) and we drove past the old internment camp for refugees? I think that's been preying on my mind ever since. Most of the time I don't think about it, but from time to time that image comes back and I wonder, about your parents and all the others, about how they must have felt about the British imprisoning them after the horror they had been through with the Germans. I would think it's something that has left its mark on Israelis.

You say Dovid is arrogant. The few Israelis I have met have all had something of that in them, and yet it's not what I would think of as a Jewish trait. So has that come about with nationhood? Have all these years of fighting for your land, after the thousands of years of persecution, made you like that? Well, not you personally, that's for sure. But even Avrom - I would say he has that arrogance, only in his case because he has such charm you don't feel offended by it. Well, I don't.

I haven't seen much of him recently. I don't know what he's up to but I keep pretty busy as you can imagine.

You were asking about Julia. I wish I knew what to tell you. Sometimes I think she's sinking, then suddenly she seems to pick up and I get hopeful, then she sinks again. She has been very tired lately and I've been quite worried. I think something is troubling her. Of course, that's silly because who wouldn't be troubled with her illness, but I mean something else. I don't know what. I've spoken with her Consultant about the prognosis and all he can do is shrug his shoulders. I don't mean this personally but really, I sometimes wonder about doctors and whether it's all guesswork.

Anyway, I spent last weekend with her and at first she seemed a little better, but I noticed things I haven't seen before. Her concentration is poor, which is sad because she is quite a bright person (or was) and I think she knows this is happening to her. Of course she knows, that's not what I mean. I mean she can see the progression. Perhaps that's the problem with being so bright - she can analyse her own deterioration. Sometimes she shakes, and I see her trying to stop, as much out of embarrassment as anything. All I can do is put my arms round her. It's not much, is it? I know she's dying, and so does she. She has tried to talk to me about that and I can't. Am I a coward? Yes, I must be. Here I am, a soldier, I've killed men, but that was in the heat of battle. To watch someone dying and know there's nothing you can do, that's hard. To be honest some weekends I take the cowardly way out and stay in New York.

I shan't write any more for now.

All my love

Monty

Is he being disingenuous when he says he stays in New York? He was living in Washington at this time, with Julia. Was it his way of trying not to tell too many lies, because he was after all travelling to New York regularly to meet Avrom. I even wondered, reading this letter, whether he wasn't getting into the deception business a little too enthusiastically - getting carried away with it, even with Deborah. Is that unfair of me?

The operation at KTX wasn't going well. Avrom was becoming concerned about how long it was taking to obtain any information. Monty was picking up bits and pieces, a word here, a rumour there, but nothing they could act on. They needed contact names, delivery dates, product details, and as things stood Monty was as far away from getting all these as he was when he started. Victor wasn't giving anything away. He was giving Monty assignments that seemed useful but weren't really, and Monty knew that. Was Victor testing him? He would have been foolish not to.

Avrom tried to hide his impatience but Monty could feel it, and he was upset because he felt he wasn't doing his job. It was the first time in his career that he felt quite helpless. On one trip to New York he asked for an appointment with the Secretary General and talked over his concerns with him. He told him about his wife and spent half an hour just unburdening himself while his boss listened attentively. He came away with no answers but felt better anyway for having talked about it.

New York
28th September 1992

Dear Deborah

You are a wicked woman for suggesting we have a holiday together, and I am a wicked man for wanting to say yes. Sadly, I simply can't. I'm completely swamped by work just now and I can't take any leave. I wish I could, I promise.

In fact I'm taking just a couple of days, to make a long weekend, but it's for something important (what am I saying? - seeing you is important). Rosie has been having some trouble at the university and I've promised we'll take a weekend out somewhere to have a long father and daughter talk. Obviously we can't have the conversations on the telephone a father would normally have with his daughter, so I feel this will help us to get back together. I don't know what it's about but I must give her some time to tell me in her own way.

As long as you and I don't talk about the things we can't have, like a holiday together, I put it out of my mind. But now, because you brought the subject up, I have the kind of regrets I don't usually allow myself to have. You say life is too short - well I agree with you, absolutely. But that doesn't change anything. Sometimes we just can't change the way things are.

And by the way. I just want to remind you that I love you.

Monty

Reading these letters I could feel the pressure both Monty and Deborah were under at this time, and my sympathy for their situation was greater than ever. Deborah's situation was different from Monty's though. Her marriage was effectively over, so it was not unreasonable that her thoughts should be on the man she had loved for so long. But Monty's wife did still love him. If anything, she loved him more now. That might, of course, have been a natural reaction to her mortality, but I don't mean to be uncharitable when I suggest that.

Julia's condition seems to have deteriorated quite rapidly now. But in the short term it wasn't Monty's most pressing problem. Even 'Operation Swordfish' became unimportant when it came to a problem with Rosie.

New York
7th September 1992

Dear Deborah

I'm writing again quickly to tell you what has happened. I mentioned I was taking Rose away for a few days. Well, by the time I got to Gallaudet to pick her up it was too late.

Apparently, Rosie had been going out with a boy called Jake Burmester, a farmer's son from Wisconsin. He was by all accounts a little emotionally unstable and when she told him she wanted to end the relationship it seems to have tipped him over the edge. Anyway, he rowed himself out to the middle of the lake and shot himself. He didn't make a very good job of it and they found him before he could bleed to death, but he is in a very serious condition. Naturally, Rosie has taken it pretty badly. I'm taking her over to England to her mother - we can decide at some time whether she will come back.

Well, I must stop here and get this in the post. I've packing to do and a prescription to pick up for Rosie before we set off for the airport. I'll call you when I get back

Love

Monty

New York
25th September 1992

Dear Deborah

Since I spoke to you yesterday I've had a fax from Rosie and she's fine. Of course, she could be suppressing it, but I get the impression she's dealing with this rather well. She's tremendously strong. In fact I'm rather pleased with what's happened - I don't mean to the poor boy. That certainly wasn't Rosie's fault. I know she wouldn't mess someone around. By the way, he's out of danger and should recover fully, from the wound if not from my daughter! It seems that Israel isn't the only country where they have expertise with gunshot wounds.

When we got to England Chloe met us at the airport. She made a huge fuss, implying it was my fault, as ever. Anyway, Rosie's gone down to stay with my father. They get on terribly well together, but then everyone gets on well with Dad, even Chloe. Actually, it's strange because I didn't tell her we were coming. I didn't particularly want her to meet us. I assumed my father had called her but he said he didn't. His memory isn't what it was, so there might be some doubt, but I have a feeling he would remember something like that. It's a mystery.

As you can see, I'm back in my office, saving the world from my desk. Not for long though. My battalion, if that's what it still is, are going to Canada for exercises and I've wangled an *invitation to join them. It will be better than a holiday. It's only a week, but it's exactly what I need. I expect a nice long letter from you when I get back.*

Love

Monty

When I read this my first thought that it hadn't been long since Monty had told Deborah he didn't have time to see her, so telling her about Canada was perhaps a mistake. He did go to Canada but it wasn't with his battalion. I suppose it ties in with his style - trying to make a lie contain some truth to salve his conscience.

He told a different story to Victor Kurtanjek, something about making contact with the British military attaché in Ottawa, who was an old friend of his from the Procurement Department at the Ministry of Defence.

The truth was he was meeting an old friend, but not a Briton, a Russian. Actually, Grigor Drixelius wasn't even Russian, he was Lithuanian. He had been the Soviet attaché in Amman the same time as Monty had been there. At that time, whilst Britain was supporting the Jordanian Army against Israel, the Soviets were supplying Egypt with arms and expertise. Monty and Drixelius had therefore got to know each other in the short time the former was there, and they had continued to bump into each other, like you would in their small specialised world, over the years. At the break up of the Soviet Union Drixelius returned to his native country and became a senior figure in the small Lithuanian Army.

He had been due to travel to Canada to see some new weaponry being developed by a local company which he was interested in for Lithuania; when Monty called him he wasn't especially surprised and happily arranged to meet in Ottawa. He still had many contacts in the Russian armed forces, including a number of officers who were not completely happy about the new position Russia found itself in. He was just the man Monty needed to talk to.

Monty's memoirs for the day he got back simply say that the meeting went well. He travelled directly to New York afterwards to see Avrom; he went by train, partly because Avrom told him to (if anyone was following him this was an unlikely way to travel). But he was happy to follow Avrom's instruction, because he had been on more aeroplanes in his life that one man has a right to, as he put it. And a leisurely train journey down the east coast, with the autumn colours starting to paint that picture that is peculiarly New England, he found deeply relaxing. It gave him time to sit in the observation car, drink coffee, and listen to people chatter about unimportant things while the red and gold canvas moved slowly past.

He thought about Deborah, how much he would have loved her to be with him right there and then, to share this with her, what a waste it was that she wasn't. And he thought about Rosie, and his father, and the Army and KTX Industries and Avrom and wondered what the hell he was doing. Then, for some reason, he thought about Mr Wilson. He didn't think anything in particular - he just wondered. His entry for that week finished with 'Mr Wilson' followed by a large question mark. Whoever he was he hadn't been a problem to Monty, but at the same time Monty knew he was out there somewhere, watching him. Mr Wilson wasn't going away, and Monty felt vaguely uneasy. That was strange, because he had far more pressing matters to worry about, both in his work and with his personal life, but still he couldn't shake the worry off.

Jerusalem
October 6, 1992

Mr Dearest Monty

You should get this letter when you get back from your exercise. I've written a paper for the WHO and I'm going to Geneva next week to present it. Then I'll be in New York to attend a meeting of some committee I'm on to present it again to UN health ministers. So, my love, you had better be there. I'll call you when I arrive.

I can't wait. I didn't need to say that, did I? Or did I?

All my love

Deborah

New York
15th October 1992

Dear Deborah

I'm sending this letter to the secretariat office which is arranging your meeting, so you get it when you arrive. I don't know if I shall be able to meet you, because something has happened. Julia is dead.

I got back to New York from Canada and there was a message waiting for me to go straight down to Washington. By the time I arrived it was too late. I'm still not clear what happened, but apparently she had some kind of attack while she was going down the stairs. She fell and knocked herself out. She never regained consciousness. They had her on a life-support machine at the hospital for three days but I knew it was the end. They asked for my permission to switch the machine off and it was the hardest decision of my life. It would have been so much easier to refuse, to keep her alive and not face the future. But that would have been selfish. Victor, her brother, was angry with me for not consulting him, but they weren't close and I didn't see any reason to. I was her husband and only I could take that decision. Not that it was real decision anyway - what choice was there?

I've been sitting here at my desk (I'm back in New York now) trying to think what to say, to tell you what I feel. But I can't do that, because I don't know. I won't deny it has come as a shock.

Somewhere in my mind I had the notion it was going to be a long, slow death for Julia. That's what it's like, isn't? We keep our loved ones alive, at any cost to us or them, rather than let them go. And I had always assumed that would happen. But fate took a hand and suddenly it's not like that at all. Well, in that case I'm glad. Not that she's dead, not at all, but that fate did take a hand. I must tell you I loved her, and I sometimes thought I wished she could die in some better way than that. I even asked myself if I would help her, you know, later on, if she asked me to. I thought I would.

I've often thought about my own death and decided I want nothing better than a soldier's death. I know that sounds silly but it's true. A bullet that you don't see coming, you go just like that. Of course many soldiers don't have that luck. You can be wounded in battle and die slowly and painfully. Or you could get what happened to Issy.

Look, I hope I will see you, maybe just for dinner before you fly back, and we can talk. Call my office.

Love

Monty

They did indeed meet, just for dinner, and Deborah flew back to Israel. I imagine it was a sombre meeting, even awkward. One can imagine the conflicting feelings both of them must have been having, the guilt but at the same time not wanting to waste the precious few hours they had.

Monty saw Deborah off at the airport and immediately drove to Washington for Julia's funeral. The following day, he kept an appointment with her lawyer. There were two surprises.

The first was that Julia had owned eight per cent of the stock of KTX Industries and had left these in her will to her husband. The first thing that occurred to Monty was that he was now a shareholder in a company that was likely to be prosecuted in due course by the federal government.

And there was a letter. It was in a stout manila envelope, with the lawyer's seal closing it. Monty slipped it unopened into his coat pocket, thanked the lawyer and left. The envelope stayed where it was on the way back in the cab to the house, but he could feel it there, feel its importance. But Monty was a master of self-control. He only opened it when he sat on their bed, the one he had shared only infrequently with his wife for a long time. He broke the lawyer's seal and opened the envelope, only to find another inside, this one with his name written in Julia's hand.

Washington DC
June 15, 1992

My Dear Monty

I am writing this while I still have the strength, because what I have to say to you cannot be dictated.

Dearest Monty, how can I tell you my feelings? I hope you know I love you. You have been a good husband to me but I have not been much of a wife to you. One of the hardest things about this illness is knowing that it ties you to me, without giving you what any man has a right to expect from marriage. I don't just mean when we make love. That has always been very special for me and I want you to know you are the loveliest, kindest man. But I mean also the whole spectrum of married life. I haven't been there for you when you get back from work and you've had to drag down here at weekends. I can only say I'm sorry.

I know you would have liked more children. I always thought I would have a family, but it wasn't to be. You at least have Rosie and I think she is a lovely girl. You can be very proud of her. Please say good-bye to her from me. I have left her something in my will.

I am leaving you my shares in KTX, more about which later. The house is yours too. If you ever marry again I would like to think you might live in it and be happy. My family are wealthy enough, I feel no need to leave anything to them.

Since my father died I have had less involvement with the company. That has been Victor's doing - he is power-crazy. I have things to tell you now about him and the company that I hope you will be able to make use of. First, I should explain that I know what you have been doing. I wondered for a while why you suddenly changed your mind after all those years and resigned your commission in the Army. Then one night you said some things in your sleep, and I started to put it together. Don't worry, I have told no-one. In fact, I am going to help you. Why would I do that? Because I don't approve of what my father did, and what Victor is doing. We are American citizens. This country gave us a home and we have thrived here. If you do that, you have to accept the law of the land. I want you to stop Victor.

You can't be involved in a company for as long as I have and not learn anything about it, no matter how much secrecy there is. People came to the offices, that sort of thing. I can tell you for sure that KTX is selling components for nuclear weapons to Russia. They are made in a special department in the high-security wing. I know you have been in there – many people have - but very few people know what is made there. Even the staff involved in development and manufacturing don't know who the customers are though. That is where Victor has been clever. KTX makes parts for the US military and you would simply assume these are going to them as well. So the manufacturing and despatch are completely separate, so no-one makes that connection. The components they send to Moscow are actually very small. They are sent first to a company called USCOM in Norwalk, Connecticut. They make specialised circuitry for computers and they have an export licence to sell to the Russians. They solder the special components onto a circuit-board which goes into a spare slot in each system they build. No-one would ever think to look at them, but they're not even connected. That's about all I know, except for one other thing.

The contact in Moscow is called Brig Stewart. I don't know anything about him, but I guess he's American with a name like that. I sincerely hope this helps you in your task, and that you manage to stop Victor. If that results in KTX closing, your shares in the company will become worthless, but I know you and I know you would not let that stop you.

My dearest Monty, it only remains for me to thank you. No woman could have asked for more than you have given, and I do thank you for being my husband, and I am sorry I have to leave you. I don't know when that will be but we both know it must come sooner rather than later. I wish you happiness and health. I don't believe there is anything after this - it would be nice to believe we will be together again one day, but it's not true. My Catholic faith doesn't extend to that.

Well, good-bye again.

With love

Your devoted wife, Julia

This letter was not in fact with the others when they were given to me; it had been kept by Monty's solicitor in London. I tracked it down through his daughter Rosie and I had to obtain special permission to include it. I felt it was a vital piece in the jigsaw of his story.

There is no record in his memoirs of how he reacted to the letter. I can only imagine, and I will share my thoughts here with the reader because I don't feel I can continue with his story unless I do. I, remember, have met the people in his life, not of course Deborah, but Rosie and her husband, Yael, and others. I believe I must give you the fullest picture I can, otherwise, as a biographer, I am not fulfilling my duty.

Anyone in Monty Sutherland[1]s position would have been overcome with emotion. I don't think for a minute that his love for Deborah changed that. Can one man love two women? It's an ancient riddle, and in my experience women tend to ridicule the notion as an excuse for promiscuity. Well, Monty could not remotely be called promiscuous. He was faithful to his first wife, Chloe and also to Julia, in the physical sense. Yes he loved another woman but what, in fairness, did he ever do about it?. At the risk of boring the reader with my own moral interpretation of it, was his love for Deborah unfaithfulness? Did he love Julia less for it? All I am going to say is that I don't think so, and I am going to ask you, in honour of a very courageous man, a good man, to give him the benefit of the doubt.

Monty's first practical reaction to the letter, sitting there in his bedroom, was to put a call through to Vilnius. They said Lieutenant-General Drixelius was unavailable but would call back. Then he changed, went down to the kitchen and cooked. He knew who Brig Stewart was, but he wanted to be absolutely sure, and he didn't want anyone else to know he was checking. He found it amusing that

Julia hadn't made the connection.

He ate his lunch at leisure and as he put down his knife and fork the phone rang. It was late evening in Lithuania, but Grigor Drixelius sounded like he didn't mind. Friends don't, and right now Monty needed all the friends he could find. Grigor confirmed that the man in question, Brigadier Alexander Stewart, was the military attaché at the British embassy in Moscow. He didn't ask why Monty wanted to know, or why he found it necessary to ask an officer in the Lithuanian Army when he could easily have called London. Monty thanked him and, grateful for the lack of questions, put the phone down.

He and Alex Stewart had been in Olongwe together, at the UN mission. Monty was pretty sure he remembered it was Alex who had taken his letter, the first he ever wrote to Deborah, to the post office in the capital. His career had been as successful as Monty's; both men had made Brigadier at what would be considered an early age in peacetime.

Monty knew what he had done to get there, but what had Alex done? He needed to know, because he needed to know if his old friend was acting on orders, or ... well he didn't want to think of the alternative. In his entry for the day his final sentence is a question. How could he find out? If Alex was acting officially, then Monty was getting into something he clearly was not intended to know about. If the International Atomic Energy Agency didn't know, it seemed unlikely it was above board, but Monty could not assume the British government was playing by the rules. Why would they be helping an American company supply components for nuclear weapons to Russia? Whichever way he looked at it, it didn't make sense. The only alternative was that Alex Stewart was involved in some private operation, in which case Monty should simply hand the matter over to the authorities. But he had to be sure first. If this was a government operation he wasn't supposed to know about, he was experienced enough to know he was likely to live longer if he walked away from it.

He took a chance, a calculated one, which paid off. He called Chloe's father. Brigadier Rainsford, he knew, still had contacts. Monty asked him for personnel information on Alex Stewart, nothing he shouldn't be given, just a bit of background. He said it was for the Secretary General of the UN, who was interested in him, hinting he might be offered Monty's job. Brig Rainsford seemed to swallow that story and in very short order (actually, had Monty thought about it, abnormally quickly) sent a resume by fax to Monty in Washington. They chatted briefly about Chloe and about Rosie. Monty tended to forget, partly because he rarely asked about her, that Rainsford was his child's grandfather.

There was another question in his mind. It had been there for a while but he had never given the time to think it through. It was like a nagging toothache that you don't get fixed because there are other, more important, things to worry about. Now it nagged again. If an American company was supplying critical parts to the Russians, with or without the connivance of the British government, why was that of concern to Israel? It was possible that Avrom Mandelstam was 'on loan' from the IDF as some kind of expert, but he considered that relatively unlikely. No, it was far more likely that the Israelis had an interest in whatever was going on. But if Monty did figure it out at this stage, he didn't confide it to his memoirs.

Washington
17th November 1992

Dear Deborah

First, let me apologise for the very brief time we had together and also for not being very good company. Julia's death has left me with mixed feelings. I hope you will not mind if I tell you the truth - which is that I might have loved her more than I thought. Is that what happens when someone dies? Dare I ask - did you feel like this when Issy died?

Well, if I did, it no longer matters. It's important to me that she felt I had been a good husband. I did try. It's just that I don't know that I really was. My work took me away too much, and even when I came to the UN I couldn't be with her as much as I should have been. My thoughts right now are how very unfair it is. She should have had more than she got, but then one could say the same about Issy. They say the good die young. I don't know if that's true, or if it's just something they say to find some rationale for it. I think we die when we die, there's no reason, there's no right or wrong, that's just how it is. That's a soldier's view, perhaps. In war thousands, millions die, and we shrug our shoulders and move on. This is where people start talking about God, and sadly I can't do that. It's not the usual argument (you know, 'If there were a god this sort of thing wouldn't happen.') It's just that well, I have never discussed religion with you (is that *because we have different backgrounds, or just that when we meet we've always got better things to talk about?). But I did use to think about it and for years, when I was younger, I wasn't sure, you know, the God thing. Then, I can't remember when, the answer came to me.*

The question isn't whether there is a god - people always ask that and it's the wrong question. What they should be asking is whether it is reasonable to consider even such a proposition as a god. If you ask that question, the only reasonable answer is no. Ergo, the whole proposition on which every world religion is based is a nonsense. Julia believed - her family are practising Catholics. And because I didn't, she called me an atheist, but I'm not. An atheist is someone who doesn't believe in the Judaeo-Christian god, as far as I can make out. Well, I do believe in him. I'm sorry that's probably confusing. What I mean is, he exists, because Judaism and Christianity exist. People create gods, therefore those gods exist. They don't have to be real, or even sensible, to exist. So Julia's god exists, but as an idea, not as reality. And therefore it doesn't matter - what people believe never does any harm, does it? It only does that when they demand that other people believe the same thing. In Europe we have a history of two thousand years of wars and persecution for that very reason.

So on the one hand I think, well if people want to worship gods that's their problem, but on the other I do concern myself with the extremes of hatred generated by such belief. In my own country we see the everlasting battle between two forms of the same religion, Christianity, something started by a king called Henry VIII five hundred years ago, and still being played out today in Ireland, with no less venom.

There I go, another of my history lessons! Anyway, at least now you know my feelings. I believe your own are not much different, are they?

On a more practical note, now that Julia is no longer here, any relationship I have had with her family is going to be reduced. If we had had children there would have been an ongoing connection, but we didn't so I don't feel any good reason to have a lot to do with them. Her brother Victor is a nasty piece of work. Even at the funeral he said things that frankly were unkind. I know Julia didn't like him - she said as much in a letter she left me. Since his father died he has got worse. One day he will develop into a full-grown megalomaniac and then God help us (God? Dear me, what am I talking about?). Anyway, Julia was a minority shareholder in the company and she left that shareholding to me, so if I keep it I shall always have to have something to do with him. That might, on reflection, be a reason to sell them.

She left some money for Rosie too, which I must say was terribly kind of her. Rosie will never go short, but that will set up a good fund for her later in life. By the way, Rosie is back at university now. She came over for the funeral and we decided she should start again. She seems to have put the business with that boy behind her.

She was in no way to blame, and I think she's worked through her feelings of guilt now. I'm glad she's more settled. Julia's death upset her badly, particularly coming so soon after her boyfriend, but she is remarkably resilient. I think I've mentioned before, she's studying psychology at the university (she grew out of the maths thing) - well, I have seen a change in her own psychology since she started. She was always self-assured, but now she has an extra dimension, a confidence that comes not just from her personality but from a greater understanding of the world. One subject we never discussed while she was growing up was her own feelings about being born deaf. I didn't know whether that was a good thing or not. Now, though, she does talk about it and I'm pleased at her attitude. I thought it would be just shrugging it off (it's a bad habit she has, instead of dealing with things. I wonder who she inherited that trait from?). But instead she seems to have developed a deeper understanding of why she is deaf. I know some people, particularly the religious ones, find a rationale for it, as I suppose anyone might with a handicap (and there are much worse things than being deaf). When I say 'why she is deaf' I don't mean in the religious sense. She accepts there is no 'why', it just is. Instead, I mean, well, I don't know what I mean. She just seems to have found some sense in it.

Rosie has been a great support to me since Julia's death, even though I could tell she needed help herself. I suppose we supported each other. So she's back at her studies and that's one less thing for me to worry about.

My other news, well not news exactly because no decision has been taken, is that I'm thinking of leaving the United Nations. It's been good, but now I'm on my own again I feel the need for a change. I've been in contact with the Ministry of Defence in London and they are considering a posting for me. Anyway, as I say, there's no decision yet.

Do write and tell me all about Israel and help me think about the future, not the past.

Love

Monty

Jerusalem
December 4, 1992

Dear Monty

I've just read your letter for the third time, because I wanted to be sure what you said. I was pleased we had at least some time to see each other, and I am truly sorry it was under such circumstances. I promise you I understand about Julia. I sense you feel awkward admitting to me that you loved her, but you don't have to. You would not have married her if you hadn't loved her.

I believe there are many kinds of love. I loved Issy in a different way from Dovid, and even men I knew when I was single I thought I loved, and maybe in a way I did, but it has to be a special kind of love to want to marry someone. I believe you had that for Julia, and for your first wife. And despite that I believe you love me. It's a different kind of love again.

When you think about all the years we have known each other, there has been love for most of that time. I don't know if we are ever going to find another kind of love, the kind you have when you marry someone, because I don't now what the future holds for us, but I am happy with what we have now. And I don't feel guilty about loving you, even when Julia was alive. That might simply be because we never did anything about it (as much as I might have liked to, but really I shouldn't say that). But actually I think it's more than that. If you have two children you can love them both, even in different ways, and not have a favourite. Well, I think the kind of love we are talking about can be shared. Ideally, I suppose we should love just one person for the whole of our lives, but in my experience life isn't like that. After all, if you can fall in love again after a death or divorce, why shouldn't you do it without those things?

And talking about divorce, I can't say for sure but I think Dovid and I are going in that direction. I think I have been trying to believe what I want to believe, that we can carry on, but we can't. It's partly because of Yael that I have tried for so long, but also because I don't like to admit defeat. I feel there is some shame in a failed marriage. I know no-one these days thinks that really, but for me personally that is how it feels.

You say you might leave the United Nations. Will the Secretary General let you go? I know he particularly wanted you there. And where will you go? Please, not somewhere where you might get shot at. You're too old! Let some of the younger soldiers have a chance instead. Go somewhere nice and safe and cosy, like an embassy. You couldn't get hurt doing that, could you?

Well, my love, remember I am thinking about you. Make the right decisions, and write and tell me what they are.

All my love

Deborah

and caught a cab straight back into the city, where he met Avrom in a Jewish restaurant.

Moscow
24th March 1993

Dear Deborah

At last I am in my new home and can write to you. You should be able to address your letters here at my apartment.

Not much to report so far. I've spent a few days being shown round the place by my predecessor. You won't believe who it is - Alex Stewart. Do you remember, back in Olongwe, he was there with me? No, I don't suppose you do. He's done well for himself and he's a Brigadier, like me. Considering Alex has probably never been shot at in his entire military career, that's not bad going.

I'm going to be kept pretty busy. I don't need to tell you that the Russian Federation and NATO have a fairly difficult relationship right now, so it's my job to keep things sweet. Well, at least to stop the politicians mucking it up completely. It feels strange being in the one country I spent all those years training and preparing to fight, but that's the world we live in, isn't it? Actually, I shouldn't say this but Russian troops aren't anywhere near as scary as we thought. When you see the parades in Red Square you think they look invincible but that's just for show. The average squaddy from Siberia wouldn't stand up for long against our men (or yours, come to that). It's not their fault - they just don't get paid enough for one thing, and their equipment's not up to *scratch. I think part of it is the difference between a professional army, like ours, and a conscripted one. I know your is also conscripted, but you have a state of war, which is different.*

Anyway, I think this is just the job for me. It's a relief to put America behind me, with all it means. I won't forget Julia, ever, but it just feels right to have a fresh start. Mind you, if I could have chosen a time to come to Moscow, it would not have been March. In Washington or London we would be looking forward to spring, but here it's still in the grip of winter.

Still, I have a comfortable flat and they've given me a car with a driver, so I'm pretty well set up. I've even thought of having Rosie over here in the summer. Well, that's all for now.

Love

Monty

Jerusalem
April 12, 1993

Dear Monty

So you did it! You just packed up and went to Russia. I'm impressed. All the time I have known you where have I been? Israel. OK, the trips to Geneva and America, but you, you pack up and go, really go, not like a tourist. Don't you miss home? Perhaps I shouldn't have asked that - it will make you homesick.

I must tell you about a strange thing. A friend of mine, she's a doctor here at the same hospital, her name is Leah Orlovsky, well she was coming back from Moscow the other day - she still has family there. She saw Avrom on the plane. She didn't say anything to him, I don't know why, but she's shy and perhaps that's all it was, but she's certain it was him.

There's no reason why Avrom shouldn't be in Moscow. I told you a long time ago I don't ask about his work. But it just seems like a coincidence to me that as soon as you arrive there, he's there also. He's in America when you are, and England too. Is this coincidence, or is there something I should know about you and my brother? Listen, if I shouldn't be asking, please tell me, but I love the two of you and I think I have a right.

Talking of the men in my life, my father has had a slight heart attack. Nothing too serious, but it's a warning. I want him to move into a home but he won't, so instead I have to worry about him. Why do parents treat their children like that? Anyhow, it gets me out of

Jerusalem - I go to Netanya as much as I can just to check up on him. I tidy the apartment and bake for him but he knows I'm keeping watch on him. Yael comes with me sometimes. She's a good girl, and my father is always delighted to see her. As if I need to say, Dovid doesn't come. I don't know what to say about him. He seems to have lost interest in life. I think I've been a disappointment to him. I don't see what is going to happen to our marriage - we talk sometimes about separating but really, I can't see it. You might say I should just go, but I can't explain it - it's not that simple.

Well, enjoy Moscow. I shall start knitting you a pair of warm gloves, ready for next winter.

Love

Deborah

Monty and Avrom were both worried about the latter being seen on the flight from Moscow to Tel Aviv. It couldn't be helped, but they tried to limit any damage. Monty telephoned Deborah from a secure line at the embassy. Trying not to sound too concerned about it, he asked her to say nothing. He hinted that they were in fact working together but that there was nothing to worry about, it was fairly routine stuff to do with the United Nations and no, no-one was going to get shot at, and yes, he would look after her brother and he also promised to look after himself. Deborah pretended not to be anxious and Monty pretended to believe her.

They knew the time available for the operation was limited. Monty was not a professional operative and, although Avrom was, the incident on the plane was a timely reminder that the smallest mistake would jeopardise their plans. Yet again there is a note in Monty's memoirs about the wisdom of entrusting such a serious matter to him, rather than putting a team, say, from MI6 on it. In fact that was happening in parallel, unbeknown to either of them, but no-one had the kind of access that Monty had. He was the right man in the right place at the right time. His prior heroism might have clouded certain people's judgment of his capabilities but at the end of the day, as is often the case in these things, you have to use whatever limited means you have. The British secret services have a long and honourable history of success with amateurs even as recently as the second world war. It must also be remembered that at this point no-one had any real idea of what the threat was.

And as is often the case in these things, their first breakthrough in Moscow came about by chance.

They knew they were going to need help if they were to find anything out, but who could they turn to? If this was an official Russian operation, it wasn't safe to talk to anyone.

Monty put a suggestion to Avrom and, in absence of a lot of choices, it was decided to take a calculated risk. He called Grigor Drixelius in Vilnius. Would Drixelius help? Why should he, without knowing what was going on? But Monty had a trump card, and he used it now. Before he left New York, the Secretary General had given him a letter asking that anyone who was asked should render Brigadier Montgomery Sutherland any and all assistance, the consequences of which the UN would be responsible for. When Monty told Drixelius about the letter, the Lithuanian agreed at once to fly to Moscow.

When Monty met him at the airport and introduced Avrom, it was the first and last time Drixelius showed any surprise, and even that was brief. This was a man you could trust. What he was being asked to do was to ferret among his contacts in the military, without arousing suspicion, for someone who could be trusted to work with them. It took him a few days, but in due course he met them at Monty's apartment with not a man but a woman, whom he introduced simply as Marfa. Marfa was a major in the military police. She had a Russian father and a Lithuanian mother. Grigor trusted her. That was good enough for Monty, but Avrom wasn't happy about extending the circle of people who knew about this, especially people who historically had not been friends to the Jews. Despite his unease, he recognised that their options were limited, and since he trusted Monty's judgment he went along with it.

Marfa proved to be the perfect ally. Avrom resolved to co-operate fully with her and switched on his charm. The two of them became friends in no time, and Monty could only smile at this turn of events. Marfa's rank was sufficiently high that she signed herself out on an undercover job, commandeered a car for them and, to avoid bringing anyone else in, drove it herself. Now they were ready.

The problem was, they had a team ready for ... what? They needed a lead and it was difficult to see where it might come from. It came out of the blue. Marfa was driving Avrom to Monty's flat one morning and, for no good reason, listened in to the city police frequency on her radio. What she heard meant nothing to her, and Avrom didn't speak Russian so he had no idea what it was. But she just happened to mention the message to him and he made her stop the car to listen to the next few messages.

To the south of the city, on a waste dump, some scavengers had found what appeared to be brand-new computer equipment. They had tried to sell it and somehow or other the local police had got to hear about it. It wasn't important, just a routine call for a van to come to the local station and collect it. Without waiting to tell Monty, Avrom had Marfa drive straight to the police station. There, she flashed her ID card and a beautiful smile; the local officers didn't care who had it and in no time they were speeding back into the city with one of the boxes in the boot of the car.

Monty, Drixelius, Avrom and Marfa ate breakfast with the computer sitting in the middle of the table. When they finished their food they cleared away and took the thing apart. The most unusual feature was that none of the components had a maker's mark, even the microchips. Where the makers' stamps had been was just a space, slightly rough to the touch, where someone had very gently gone over it with something abrasive, perhaps emery paper. And the mother board had one empty slot.

Whoever had done this had been in a hurry. As Avrom dismantled it he found first a very short piece of ribbon cable with a mark on it. It was some Japanese company, and there was nothing they could tell from it. Then they got lucky. Avrom gently prised the power supply away and underneath it, where they had probably thought no-one would ever see it, was a stamp. The maker's mark was illegible, but not the address - Norwalk, Conn.

Moscow
30th April 1993

Dear Deborah

Are you really knitting gloves for me? That I have to see! In any case, by the time you've finished them it will be summer here and I shan't need them, and I don't think I'll be here another year, well I hope not.

The little bit of work we've been doing is going well and, as promised, no-one has shot at me yet.

I've been trying to understand the situation between you and Dovid. I must say I can't imagine what it is like to live like that. I hope you know I am not a judgmental person, but it does seem odd to me to live with a man you don't love, who has been unfaithful to you. What do you get out of the relationship? Look, I'm sorry, I shouldn't say these things, but I must tell you I hope one day you and I will be together and how can I see that happening if your situation isn't going to change?

My dearest Deborah, you know I have never put you under pressure, and I don't intend to now, but I also feel entitled to express my feelings, so I hope you will forgive me.

All my love

Monty

Jerusalem
May 14, 1993

Dear Monty

I was a little surprised by the tone of your letter. I don't think you can appreciate my life - you go around saving the world but some of us have to just get on with our lives and our jobs and being parents. You don't stay in one place for long, so you don't really have a home, and I don't think you know what that means.

And you say I don't love Dovid. Even that isn't simple. Remember, you loved Julia, and I respected that. Well, my love for Dovid hasn't just gone away because of what has happened. I don't mean I love him so there is no future for you and me. I mean Dovid and I used to love each other and that has to be allowed to expire, in its own way. Even if I didn't love him, I believe he still loves me, and if only one partner still loves the other it makes a marriage hard to end. Can you understand that? And we have Yael to consider as well.

To be honest, if I thought you were ready to settle down somewhere and have a proper home, I might feel differently.

Love

Deborah

What Monty thought about this letter I don't know, because he was too busy to commit his thoughts to paper.

Now that they had the computers KTX had used to ship the circuit boards to Russia, they needed to find out who had been handling them. Marfa took the equipment that afternoon and came back with it later. She put it back on the table with a sheaf of paper. The cabinet had revealed a large number of fingerprints, most of which were useless - many people must have handled it. But there was one, imperfect, print that the Moscow city police database had found a match for. Basyr Baseyev.

Baseyev was known to the Russian Interior Ministry Police, and Marfa had pulled his file from their computer. This is what now sat on the table in front of them. She read through it quickly and translated bits to read out to the others. The police had a long-standing interest in him. A Chechen, he was known to involved with the separatist movement in his country, as some kind of fixer in Moscow. He usually kept sufficiently distant from the action to avoid too much police interest. So why had he handled the equipment himself? Moscow police had made a number of arrests in recent months. Did this indicate Baseyev was short of people to do the work for him? Or was this so secret he didn't trust anyone else?

They were working in a vacuum, and there were too many unknowns. And one of those, for Monty at least, was where Alex Stewart fitted into this. He was getting more sure now that the British Government was not involved, not with Chechen separatists. No, this was a private operation.

They needed more information, a lot more. And the only person in their small team who had access to any was Marfa. She made a telephone call to military police HQ and was given indefinite leave to work with Monty and Avrom. Obviously, other people were worried about this, even if they didn't know too much about it at this stage.

Monty spoke no Russian, but he thought he heard Marfa say something about Baseyev and Grozny. That must have been enough to ring alarm bells at headquarters.

The next thing Marfa said shouldn't have taken them by surprise but it did. Apart from Grigor Drixelius, who as a Lithuanian could not afford to get to involved, she was the only Russian speaker, and she had the authority to ask questions. She would have to go to Grozny. If Monty was surprised, Avrom was more than that. He was worried. Worried not just in a professional way - now Monty could see what was happening. In the few short days since she had arrived, Avrom had fallen for Marfa. Now Monty realised why the two of them had turned up together that morning.

He had always thought Avrom was a ladies' man, and the realisation that he and Marfa had spent the previous night together was unsurprising, but there was more. The look on his face said this woman meant something more to him. Monty hadn't looked at Marfa, not like that, and now he did and he smiled to himself. Yes, she was a very attractive woman, even, or especially, in her uniform.

No-one had command of this operation. The four of them were different nationalities, with different national interests. Drixelius, as a Lieutenant-General, outranked Monty and Avrom, who in turn outranked Marfa. Someone had to make a decision, an operational one, regardless of personal interests. And Monty had the Secretary-General's letter. He now took this out, unfolded it and placed it on the table between them. He looked at Avrom and waited. His friend hesitated, but then Monty got the look he was waiting for, the look that said he would accept his orders.

So Marfa prepared to leave for Chechnya. Her HQ sent over another car, this time with a driver, and from his appearance it was obvious he was also her bodyguard. He shook everyone's hand in silence, which might have meant he spoke no English but probably also indicated he wasn't much interested in them. Monty didn't know what danger Marfa was going into, but he liked this man's bulk and his demeanour and felt a little reassured. Like Avrom, but for a different reason, he didn't want to see Marfa hurt.

Once Marfa and her driver had left there was nothing the others could do but wait. The drive to Grozny would take some time. Grigor explained she would pick up an army escort once they crossed the border into Chechnya - that was standard practice. This would provide some level of safety but it would also make her more visible.

Drixelius was staying at his country's embassy and he retired there to work. It was no bad thing for the three of them not to be seen too much around the city anyway. Avrom did likewise - he spent the next few days at the Israeli embassy doing Monty didn't know what, which left Monty on his own with nothing to do but worry.

Moscow
30th May 1993

Dear Deborah

Are you angry with me? I'm sorry, I shouldn't have written like that. But isn't it right we should tell each other our true feelings? Look, I do understand about you and Dovid, or at last I am working on it. I suppose it's jealousy. He has you and I don't.

I completely accept your criticism about my life. It hasn't really mattered before. I suppose you could argue that if I'd had a normal job, coming home every evening, Chloe might have been faithful, but I don't think she would. It wasn't the job - after all the man she had the affair with was a soldier too.

It's true Julia didn't much like the life, but I'll never know if that would have mattered enough to be a problem. And as for Rosie, well, being away at the special school it didn't much matter where I was. So you could say I've been able to be self-indulgent and do what I wanted to do, because I didn't have the ties most men have.

But Deborah, please believe me when I say this - if you are telling me that giving up this life would bring us together, I promise you I would do that tomorrow. I have served my country, more than most men are ever asked to. I don't live for the army. If you would be with me, I would live for you. That, my darling, is my promise.

And on the subject of matters of the heart, I

probably shouldn't tell you this but I think Avrom is in love. I won't say too much about it, but he's showing all the signs. I can tell you she's Russian, and really rather attractive. I don't know if it will come to anything but I must say he could do worse. She's not Jewish - does that matter? I suppose not to you, since I'm not either.

How are those gloves coming along?

All my love

Monty

Jerusalem
April 12,1993

My Dearest Monty

I have said to you before that life is too short to wait. I don't want to wait any longer. If you are ready, I am ready. Tomorrow then.

Love

Deborah

Moscow
22nd April 1993

Dear Deborah

Do you mean it? What about Dovid? I have to complete what I am doing here. I can't say too much but I promise it is the only thing that would keep me from you. Much depends on it, including Avrom, so I ask you to believe me.

When it's over, I shall resign my commission. I will get a good pension and I'm not short anyway, not to mention what Julia left me, so I shall be a free agent, as we say.

But what about Dovid?

Love

Monty

Jerusalem
May 8, 1993

Dear Monty

Dovid doesn't live here any more.

Love

Deborah

A week passed and there had been no word from Marfa. Monty took Avrom to dinner at his favourite Jewish restaurant but couldn't cheer him up. They talked about what might have gone wrong and then they sat and ate more or less in silence.

Drixelius came round to Monty's apartment and said he would have to return to Vilnius, but that if he were needed they should call. There didn't seem to be much he could do, and a Lieutenant-General can't disappear for too long, not in a small army.

Drixelius was a cheery man, and they missed his support, just knowing he was in Moscow. Another week passed, and by now Monty had run out of sensible things to say to Avrom. He himself had duties at the embassy, and now he devoted more time to them, if only to take his mind off the situation. Without Marfa, they didn't have an operation.

Then she returned. Monty got an excited call from Avrom at his office; he couldn't leave just then as he was about to go into a meeting, but as soon as he could decently absent himself he rushed back to the apartment, where Avrom had already let himself in. He and Marfa stood up suddenly when Monty came through the door. He had obviously caught them out, and they blushed. There was no sign of the driver.

Over coffee Marfa briefed them on what she had learned in Grozny. She had gained complete access to police and army files; wherever she went people seemed to want to help. Baseyev operated from Moscow but the Russian authorities in Chechnya were well aware he was pulling the strings in Grozny, and anyone who might give them a lead in halting his activities was welcome.

Marfa had brought back with her a great deal of Intelligence and Monty was impressed. Avrom was staring at her a little foolishly and Monty decided he was out of the

Moscow
17th May 1993

My Dear Deborah

Well, things are moving nicely here, and the little bit of work I was telling you about should be finished quite soon. Then I'll get back to London and start making the arrangements to leave the Army.

Whatever happens, remember I love you. I have promised we will be together, and I will do everything in my power to keep that promise.

I am enclosing another envelope with this. I want you to promise me something. You are not to open this envelope, no matter what, unless you receive instructions to do so. I'm sorry to be secretive, but trust me.

I'll be with you soon.

All my love

Monty

I have read the contents of that other envelope, and in due course so will you, but not just now.

When Grigor Drixelius arrived from Lithuania they had one more night together to prepare for their departure for Grozny. It was to be a near-disaster.

I have some of the detail of what happened from Monty's memoirs but it is in the nature of these things that there were as many opinions about it as there were people there. After rather a lot of research, of necessity rather a long time after the event, I can offer the reader what I think is some kind of consensus, but I don't vouch for its authenticity.

So far in the story my opinion of Lt. Gen. Drixelius is that he was the sort of man you could rely on, older than the others and some kind of father figure perhaps. At least that, I think, is how he saw himself, but this is to ignore the dynamic of the group. They were rather a mixed bunch. Drixelius, a former officer in the Soviet Red Army, was now a very senior officer in the independent state of Lithuania. Why was he there? There was no love lost between his country and Russia. Lithuania had a long history of subservience to Russia and one can imagine a man in his position being rather proud and aloof when it came to dealing with the Russians. Lithuania had no interest in this operation and I have wondered if it wasn't for Drixelius an adventure, informed to some extent by the pleasure of being able to offer help to his former masters.

How did the others see him? Well, Monty would certainly have taken him at face value. They hadn't known each other well in the old days but Monty I think had a tendency to trust people. That might seem odd in someone who had worked for so long in Military Intelligence, especially in Northern Ireland where he should have known better. I suspect it was his religious upbringing to some extent, combined, one must remember, with the class into which he had been born. I would place Monty's family in the lower echelons of the upper class. They are people, I have found, who assume the best in people because they themselves know the correct way to behave.

To Marfa, Drixelius would, despite his nationality, have been someone to treat with respect simply by virtue of his rank. The Russian military conforms to the old model of the officer class. Unlike some countries (the US comes immediately to mind), the class structure in Russian society has such a long history that no political system changes it much, not Communism certainly, in which both Marfa and Grigor had grown up. Her respect for a Lieutenant-General would have been unquestioning, especially one who had served in her own army.

Avrom's attitude to Drixelius would have been somewhat different though. Israel, first of all, does not have a class structure as we understand it, and the relationship between soldiers of different ranks is very much more relaxed than a British officer, say, would recognise. Add to that Drixelius' nationality; without giving a lot of history here suffice it to say that to a Jew it would not be a plus point.

So, while Monty and Marfa would have given Drixelius respect automatically, the same did not apply to Avrom. And this was the start of the problem.

They had discussed the plan until quite late after their evening meal; a bottle of vodka had appeared from somewhere and, having said everything that needed to be said, the conversation had started to go off in different directions. The following day was Sunday, and Drixelius said he wanted to go to Mass before they set off. Drixelius, like most Lithuanians, was a Catholic, and it would have been quite normal for him to attend Mass every Sunday. Monty, being Anglican, went to Church Parade when in England, because that's what officers did, but wasn't much bothered otherwise. He didn't query Grigor's request and neither, despite her lack of religion herself, did Marfa. Avrom, however, said he didn't want to waste time when they should be getting an early start. Whether there was an undertone of contempt for Drixelius' beliefs I can't say, but certainly the latter reacted badly. He said something to Avrom about Jews; I haven't been able to get a straight story about exactly what he said but what is certain is that it went down very badly.

Avrom said something fairly aggressive and before Monty or Marfa knew what was happening they had a religious war on their hands. To Monty, in fairness, this seemed like an argument over nothing, but something Drixelius said must have struck a chord with Marfa. A product of the Communist system, her attitude to religion was one more or less of contempt. Apparently, her parents had recently returned to the resurgent Russian Orthodox Church, something they would have inherited from their own parents. But Marfa had been brought up in a society that scorned religion and that was difficult to change. It was also a society in which anti-Semitism was official policy, and that too she had absorbed unquestioningly. In fact, I don't think she had ever even met anyone Jewish before Avrom, so her prejudice was, like a lot of prejudice of all kinds, theoretical.

She had known Avrom only for a matter of days, and the man, not the Jew, had won her heart. Having fallen for him, she now had to deal with the part of him she hadn't thought about, his Jewishness, and she wasn't sure how to do that. And now here was Drixelius coming out with the standard anti-Semitic claptrap of his generation. Monty knew it for that and, whilst surprised by it, had the maturity and experience of the world to see where it came from. Marfa had neither of those things. This senior officer was saying things people in Russia often said, things she had never thought to query. But he was saying them about a man she felt something for, a man who was clearly none of the things Jews were supposed to be.

At this point Avrom looked to Marfa for support, but she couldn't give it. Not because she didn't want to but because she didn't know how to. She was ready to defend Avrom in any way he needed, but she was, sadly, entirely ignorant of the truth on this matter. She was giving Avrom the benefit of the doubt, not because she suddenly saw the truth about the lies she had taken in with her mother's milk, but because she had these feelings about him. What she could not do, though, was argue with Drixelius, both because she didn't know what to say and because she wouldn't have argued with a superior officer, even a foreign one.

Monty could see his team, and the operation, falling apart. And all because of a stupid comment. He realised then how fragile the whole thing had been. Why should this diverse bunch of people work together? Throughout history, people who appeared to coexist had suddenly and disastrously split into their historical factions and blood had flowed. He didn't have to look too far across the Irish Sea to find a prime example. How was he going to knit his people back into a team, in a short time, after some pretty nasty things had been said?

Why had Drixelius behaved so badly? Was it the drink? Should he have been professional enough to keep his mouth shut, regardless of what he actually thought? Probably, if he had been on an official mission, he would have. But again we have to remember this was some personal adventure for him and I suppose he felt less constrained by the correct way to behave. Certainly, he behaved badly and he risked the entire mission. But at the same time, was he not also a victim of the culture in which he grew up? Monty, after he overcame his own anger and frustration at what had happened, asked the same question in his memoirs. You can't blame a man for believing what he has been taught. It takes generations to change long-held beliefs that run through a society and, in my experience, racial prejudice and hatred runs through European society like a cancer.

I wouldn't even say, with respect to Monty, that he was entirely free of those prejudices. It might not have been about Jews but about, say, Asians or Blacks. It is my belief that the Army is like society in microcosm, and society is deeply racist. It was more that, because of his place both in society and in the hierarchy of the Army, he had no occasion to express what he might have thought. He probably wouldn't even have admitted to himself that he thought them. Isn't that often the way?

In any case, in that barracks in Chechnya, it was Monty's job as commanding officer to sort this out, and to sort it out quickly. He had a problem between Drixelius and Avrom, but also between Avrom and Marfa. He could appeal to Grigor to apologise and Grigor probably would, but you can't unsay what you've said. Although he was very fond of Avrom, and was pleased about what was happening between him and Marfa, he was more concerned at this point with the operation, so if they fell out it would have to be like that. Even the love he had for Deborah didn't change the way he would have to treat her brother. This was an operational matter, and Monty was thinking like a soldier and a commanding officer.

He realised there was almost nothing he could do either with Drixelius or Marfa. They were victims of their own upbringing. No, if there was a chance to save the situation it would have to be between him and Avrom. He persuaded the others to go to bed and he and Avrom talked. There is no record of exactly what was said, but I understand it was Avrom who did most of the talking. He gave Monty a history lesson and Monty sat and listened. He heard many things for the first time, and for the first time he came to understand, at least a little, what it means to be Jewish. Why, when people say the Jews should leave history behind and look forward, they are wrong. That every Jew carries the cries of his brothers and sisters in his heart, even if, for most of his life, he is deaf to them. That he carries a responsibility to those who were born and died before him, to those who will follow him. That, in the late twentieth century, there was still no country in the world where a Jew was safe from all ill-feeling or physical harm, except the one he came from originally. That after thousands of years of persecution, he would fight for that country with his last breath, because what he didn't take no-one, but no-one, was going to give him. That every Jew comes into the world with a history, one he cannot deny.

And he answered the question that Monty finally found the courage to ask him, in that darkened room in that Godforsaken place, the day before they might be going to their death. Why does the world hate the Jew?

The answer was that the world doesn't. That surprised Monty. Avrom said that anti-Semitism spread across the world with Christianity, with Monty's own religion (although in fairness Avrom was referring to the Catholic Church, not the Church of England). I hesitate to report this conversation because I myself don't know the truth of what Avrom told Monty, but it is my job as an historian to report what I do know for the reader to judge. Monty, I know, judged Avrom right. He could see the logic, that if you look at a map of the world, anti-Semitism exists where the Church exists, and not elsewhere. That the war against the Jew was a Christian war. Others, like the Arabs, might adopt it for their own purposes, but he knew enough history, going back to the Crusades, to see the truth of it.

They talked late into the night and finally Avrom talked his anger out. Monty knew that when they woke Drixelius would shrug it off as if it hadn't happened. He hoped Avrom and Marfa would talk and come to their own understanding. And he knew, now, that Avrom would do his job.

When Grigor returned from the church service, they were ready. They set off with Marfa's driver, still as silent and just as reassuring. In the boot of their car was their small amount of personal luggage and enough firepower to start a small war. Or finish one. On the road, Monty had a lot of time to think, and one of the questions he asked himself was why they were taking Drixelius with them. It had seemed a good idea at the time but now he couldn't think what it was. He concluded that Grigor was coming for the adventure. Well, he was welcome. He sat in the front next to the driver, while Monty squeezed in the back with Avrom and Marfa. He didn't disturb them. Avrom had learned enough Russian that he could have a halting private conversation with Marfa in that situation, and in any case their whispers could not have been heard above the noise of the engine. It appeared to Monty, though, that they had come to an understanding about the night before.

And why, in any case, was Avrom with them? It was the question that had been nagging him for a long time. Why was a nuclear device being shipped half way round the world, and ending up in Chechnya, of interest to the Israelis? If this was a war brewing between Russia and the Chechens, even with a small tactical nuclear weapon, that was a local matter, surely? Now though Monty could see that wasn't true. This weapon was heading south, but how far south? Was it going to stop in Grozny? If the Saudis were financing it, that was understandable. After all, Chechnya is a Moslem country and this fight had as much to do with religion as territory.

No, if the Israelis were involved in this, then they must have thought the weapon was going further, and further than Chechnya meant an Arab country, and that meant trouble, very serious trouble, for Israel. All the years Monty had known Avrom, this must have been what he was doing - tracking nuclear weapons components to Israel's enemies.

As he sat in the car, buried in his thoughts, he traced his relationship with Avrom back over the years, to the time he thought Avrom had been using him, to KTX Industries, to Avrom being there every time. Had Avrom wanted him to work for KTX? He no longer thought Deborah was involved in any way, but he started to wonder again if he had been used. He concluded that he probably had, and, to his surprise, he didn't mind. What would he have done in Avrom's shoes? There he was, with his sister's lover in a position to help him, and he took advantage of it. On reflection, Monty hadn't gone to work for KTX because of Avrom. True, Avrom might have steered him in certain directions, but it seemed to Monty that things had, well, just worked out right. The stakes were high, not just for Avrom's country but for Deborah's, and now Monty felt all right about that. He felt, more than ever, a pull towards Israel. It was in the back of that car, on the long bumpy road south, that Monty Sutherland decided that, if he came out of this alive, he would settle in Israel with Deborah.

Somewhere in southern Russia
23rd May 1993

My Dearest Deborah

I am writing this in my notebook by moonlight, because I want to tell you, right now, how much I love you.

I have a bad feeling about this whole operation. I've never felt it before, and I would always have said a soldier has no business with such things, but I feel it nevertheless. Is it because, now, I want to live?

It's dark outside and I don't know where we are. If the driver stopped and put me out of the car, I would be utterly lost and defenceless. My life is in the hands of these people; your brother, a Russian Major he has fallen in love with, a Lithuanian Lieutenant-General who thinks this is an adventure and a silent soldier, God alone knows what he's thinking.

Still, I must stop thinking about my life and focus on the operation. I believe in what we are doing. Sometimes, in the Army, you do things you don't believe in, because you're following orders, but this I didn't have to do. If we succeed, it will have been the best thing I ever did and .....

The car slowed and stopped. Ahead of them were headlights, then the sound of a door slamming, voices, boots on the road surface. Monty thought he heard Russian but couldn't be sure. Marfa had been asleep with her head on Avrom's shoulder. Now the two of them stirred. Monty grabbed his friend's sleeve and hissed at him to keep quiet. Avrom's first words might have been in Hebrew and that might have been a bad idea.

A torch shone into the car and by its light Monty could see a face, an ugly, leering one staring in at him. It took in Marfa, and just then Monty wished they were all in uniform. This was a Russian soldier - he could just make out the badge on his arm, and Monty was familiar enough with the Cyrillic alphabet to see it said Russia. The driver said something to him through the open window, and Monty remembered later being surprised at the sound of his voice, something he didn't remember hearing before, although he thought he must have. Strange, the things you recall.

Their driver handed their papers to what Monty took to be a junior officer. When he saw who they were the lieutenant snapped to attention, threw a smart salute to the car in general, and barked an order. The soldiers scuttled back to their vehicle. The driver took the papers back and they were on their way.

Marfa explained that all vehicles on this road were stopped and searched by the military. It was just routine. It happened twice more.

Once they were on their way Avrom and Marfa fell asleep again. Monty couldn't see too much but he could see enough and he wondered what would happen to these two. Would they come through this, and if they did, was there a future for them? Or was he misjudging the situation? Perhaps it wasn't like that, perhaps it was just two people who were thrown together by their circumstances, nothing more. He hoped not.

As he let his mind wander, once again he started to wonder about Alex Stewart. He thought about the one issue he hadn't been able to resolve in his mind - who posted Alex to Saudi Arabia? If the financing for this weapon was coming from Saudi, wasn't that just putting him where he needed to be? Alex was apparently the brains behind the money, but did someone in London know that? Who had arranged the posting, and were they part of the plot or had they deliberately placed Alex in Riyadh for other reasons? Yet again, Monty had an equation with unknowns on both sides.

Who had arranged for Monty to go to Moscow and replace Alex? That was easy - Chloe's father, Brig. Rainsford. Who had been there throughout Monty's career, pushing him into certain postings, helping him with information about Alex? How had Rainsford managed to get Alex's personnel file so quickly? After all he wasn't even a serving officer. Monty was coming to a conclusion that was impossible to believe, that Chloe's father was somehow involved in a plot to supply nuclear weapons to an Arab country. If he was, was there any chance that it was official, that the government wanted somehow to change the nuclear balance in the Middle East? That, to Monty, seemed unlikely in the extreme. The Foreign Office was notoriously hostile to Israel and always had been, but no, not that. Could it be an operation so deeply undercover that people in government didn't even know about it, like the Iran-Contra affair in the US? Sitting in this car in the middle of nowhere, almost anything seemed possible, but when Monty thought back to the quiet corridors of Whitehall, the ordered existence that was the reality in Britain, he decided he was getting carried away.

If Brigadier Rainsford, his erstwhile father-in-law, was involved, Monty wanted to believe there was a more reasonable explanation. At that moment, though, he couldn't think of one. Ultimately, he had to be aware that this entire operation could have been set up for some purpose he didn't know about. Was he being sent into some kind of trap? He couldn't answer that question other than by going and finding out. Suddenly, those four people in the car with him seemed like the only friends he had. Even their silent Russian driver. He was confused and tired, and having come to a dead end, he fell asleep.

As Monty awoke he was aware the car was slowing. It was getting light, and forcing his eyes open he could see there was activity outside. They were approaching what appeared to be a border post. He peered at his watch and did a quick calculation. This must be Chechnya. The five of them bundled out of the car and breathed in the chill morning air, which felt a lot better than the stale air they had been breathing all night. It seemed they were expected here. They were ushered into the guardhouse where there was hot coffee and, more importantly just now, toilets and a shower.

Monty felt almost human again as they got back into the car. Their driver had taken care of the vehicle, refuelled it, cleaned the filth off the windscreen, checked the oil and tyres. But he didn't look like he had taken advantage of the shower.

Now, they had an escort. Not just a jeep, but a truckload of soldiers as well. Monty wondered if this was a good thing, or just a bigger target for some Chechen with a rocket-propelled grenade and a hatred of Russians. Still, no-one had asked his opinion, and he didn't offer it. Four hours later they rolled into what he took to be the capital.

As they drove, Marfa explained to him and Avrom that they were now in what was nominally independent Chechnya. There was still a Russian military presence there to protect Russian interests but they had no real rights in what was a sovereign state. They themselves were there on sufferance, and probably the best safeguard they had was Monty's letter from the Secretary-General of the United Nations. The average Chechen trooper would have no idea what that meant, but with any luck their officers would. She warned Monty, if he needed to show it to anyone not to let them take it away. And they would have to hope no-one wanted to search the boot. It was one thing to enter the country with permission, quite another to have a small arsenal in the car.

They stopped outside a grimy building of the kind Monty associated with the military. There was a small showing of barbed wire above the surrounding wall, and a sloppy guard who looked like he could easily be taken by surprise by a platoon from the Royal Welch Fusiliers. The party were shown directly into a briefing room, where a small group of officers, looking rather more businesslike, greeted them in Russian. Drixelius found their accent hard to understand and it fell to Marfa to interpret.

They made it clear they wanted to deal with Baseyev almost as much as Moscow did. The groups he was supplying weapons to were stirring up trouble for the authorities and they would be pleased to hand him over, dead or alive. They assured Monty that the Chechen Government was not interested in obtaining parts for a nuclear weapon and they wanted no such thing on their soil. Monty could see why this would be. If the Kremlin thought for a moment the Chechens had even one nuclear device it would be a reason to invade. He said nothing about his thoughts on the ultimate destination, but realised the presence of an Israeli on the team would give them a pretty good idea. If it did, they said nothing.

The Chechens knew most of the bomb was already in the country but hadn't been able to find it since Marfa had been there earlier. The circuit board supplied by KTX

Industries contained electronics vital to triggering the device and so it was imperative they stop it being delivered. They had Intelligence that a Brigadier Stewart had booked a flight from Riyadh in two days time and the imminent arrival of a high-ranking British officer in their country, not on official business, had aroused their suspicion. Monty was able to tell them that Alex was the paymaster, and this must mean Baseyev was coming to Chechnya to deliver the board. It gave them two days to finalise their plans. They showed Monty and his team to their quarters.

... I will always know it was right. If I die, well, that is my lot as a soldier. I am sorry I can't be there for you if that happens, and I can only ask you to understand. I will do all I can to protect Avrom for you and if I don't make it, perhaps he will find my notebook and show you this.

No more, or I shall get maudlin.

With all my love

Monty

The bed wasn't too soft and the sheets weren't exactly clean, but to Monty it was bliss and he slept the sleep of the just. The last thing he thought as he drifted off was whether Avrom and Marfa had found somewhere to be together.

By the next morning plans had already been made by their Chechen hosts. Monty and his team were not part of those plans. They would stay at the barracks and await the result of a squad of Chechen troops. Monty argued, as well as he could with Marfa interpreting his anger. Drixelius tried, but no-one could change the Chechen commander's mind. He didn't want foreigners involved in an internal operation. Monty argued that it was an international operation but it was no good. The troops would stay in radio contact with them to receive instructions but that was all. They would have to sit and wait. Monty had been a soldier long enough to know when to accept an order and keep quiet.

The team worked with the Chechens to go through the plan over and over again. There was one unknown, though, which could change it all. They knew when Brig. Stewart was arriving - the next day - but they had no Intelligence yet on Baseyev. He was being watched in Moscow but it was a long way from there to Grozny and it was anyone's guess what might happen in between. Would he come directly, or were there other plans? That issue was resolved in part that very morning when Marfa received a phone call from her HQ to inform her he had been seen leaving the city and heading north. It was a fairly routine precaution against being followed if someone was waiting for him to set out for Chechnya. It didn't fool anyone and when he turned onto the ring road, first east and then south, there was still a tail on him and after thirty minutes the tail peeled off, as instructed, to avoid any danger of being seen. It was pretty certain by then where he was going.

It's over a thousand miles from Moscow to Grozny and assuming an average speed of fifty miles an hour it would take twenty hours. Would he stop overnight, or attempt the journey in one go? The police had vehicles on the road to take sightings and keep some kind of track of him but that could easily go wrong. It did go wrong when Baseyev stopped in Kharkov and changed cars. That would have been that but for a lucky break. The new car had been stolen and the thief was now Baseyev's driver. Fortunately, the local police had the details of the car and when he was spotted by chance changing cars the system, for once, worked perfectly.

Because the car had a Moscow plate, Kharkov called there with both registrations; the duty sergeant was on his toes and matched the number of Baseyev's car up with a national request for information and within two hours Grozny had the details of the new car. This was radioed to all police vehicles on the road south and by the time the two men reached Rostov the police had a fix on them. That put them no more than six or seven hours from Grozny, barring any hold-ups at the frontier. A message was sent to the border post for the car to be allowed through with only a cursory inspection, enough not to arouse suspicion but not enough to find anything.

By now, Stewart had arrived in Grozny and had been followed to a house in a quiet location about ten miles outside the city. The team moved to a police post only a mile or so from there to be closer. All they could do now was wait. Monty was satisfied not only by the Chechens' state of preparedness but by their understanding of the situation and willingness to co-operate. He realised their insistence on handling the entire operation themselves was only reasonable. What, he thought, would the Metropolitan Police think if the CIA asked to be involved in something like this in London? And the US and Britain were allies, more than could be said or Chechnya and Britain, or come to that Chechnya and Russia. Relations between the two countries were severely strained and Monty was only too aware they had been very lucky so far.

There was little they could do while they waited, but Avrom suggested they prepare for the worst. Their car was parked at the back of the police station and the two of them nonchalantly walked round to it and, in the semi-darkness, opened the boot to check their weapons. They could hardly wander back in with automatic weapons over their shoulders, but they each put a fully-loaded pistol in their coat pockets, plus one each for Grigor and Marfa. In the last entry in his notebook before the operation kicked off, Monty expressed how good it felt to be carrying a weapon again. Now he was a soldier.

What followed has been gone over many times by the relevant authorities. Reports were written by everyone who was there, and by a few who weren't, so we will never know for sure exactly what happened. I have avoided making my own judgments and after reading the various accounts I decided I would present the reader with as much first-hand information as I had. I hope I will be forgiven therefore for presenting the reader with more detail that many historians would offer in the interest of impartiality.

What is known for sure is that Baseyev and his driver arrived at the house at about one o'clock in the morning. Of Monty's team only he was awake. He had years of experience of this kind of thing in Northern Ireland, and could stay awake longer than most men. He stirred the others and they sat round the radio listening for developments. When it was reported that Baseyev had been seen carrying a briefcase into the house Monty and the others agreed this was probably the circuit board. There was no point waiting any longer. They gave this information to the commander on the spot and left it for him to give the order. He gave his men a further ten minutes to prepare themselves, then they stormed the house. It was empty.

The cars Stewart and Baseyev had arrived in were both there, but there was no sign of anyone. The troops followed a track at the back of the house through some trees for about two hundred yards and there they found fresh tyre tracks. They radioed this information in immediately. All they could add was the direction the car appeared to be travelling in.

They had lost the suspects, who were now in a car no-one had seen, going no-one knew where. Monty cursed in frustration and they all ran for the car. They had no idea where they could look; all they could do for now was drive to the house to search for some kind of clue.

Monty, Avrom, Drixelius and Marfa piled into their car with their driver, and as many policemen as would fit crammed into another. The police car took off first, which was just as well, as no-one in Monty's car knew how to get to the house. The Russian driver had some difficulty keeping up with the Chechens, who knew the road of course, and then disaster struck. As they approached a railway line the Russian spotted a goods train coming. It would have been sensible for the Russians to have stopped but, no, they were in chase mode now and their car shot across the line just ahead of the train. Monty's car screeched to a halt, and they sat there watching wagon after wagon rumble across in front of them. Monty counted the trucks, a silly boyhood habit and Avrom later reported him telling them how many there were. Avrom couldn't remember the number though.

As the last wagon disappeared they saw the police had not waited for them. There was a car facing the other way, also waiting to cross, which was odd at that time of the night, and they all naturally peered into it as the two cars crossed the line. Monty shouted something, everyone remembers that, but they were less clear about what happened next. What Monty had shouted was Alex. Just that, one word. And for some reason their driver, to whom the name can have meant nothing, reacted with instinctive speed. He swung the wheel heavily to the left and their car struck the other.

For the sake of accuracy and hopefully some clarity, at this point I am going to quote from the reports I have been given access to from each of the members of the team, barring, for reasons that will become apparent, Monty. Copies of these reports were in due course passed from the authorities concerned to the United Nations and to the British Government.

REPORT ON THE OPERATION IN CHECHNYA

Lieutenant-General Grigor Drixelius

.... As the train passed in front of us our driver started to cross the railway line. There was another car waiting to come the other way, but I was sitting on the wrong side of the car, with the driver in my view, and could not see much of it. In the middle of the railway line someone shouted something. I don't know who it was or what they said but the driver seemed to be taken by surprise by this sudden sound, or so I thought at the time. Our car suddenly swerved and hit the other one coming towards us.

My door burst open and I fell out of the car. I believe I remember seeing, as I fell out, that our driver was slumped over the wheel, obviously injured. There was a great deal of noise, the cars, people shouting, it was very confusing to see what was happening. I fell down a small embankment and when I reached the bottom I could see our car at an angle at the top. I couldn't see any of my companions just then. But as I looked up I saw a man approach the car. The moon was behind him so I could not see his features, but he was not one of our team, that I knew. What I saw next was that he aimed a weapon at our driver's head and fired a shot.

Now, naturally, I realised that the other car must have been the people we were looking for. I could not know at the time whether they knew who we were, or whether they were simply eliminating any witnesses to their presence. I drew my weapon. He presented a perfect target because of the moonlight behind his head, and I fired two rounds. He went down immediately and I calculated that he must be dead.

My next concern was for my friends, and not knowing

how many enemy we faced. I thought there could only be three more in one car, so we were fairly evenly matched. But of course I didn't know who was alive still. I heard three more shots as I climbed up the embankment and when I got to the top I found the following.

Major Mandelstam was lying on the ground, I assumed dead. Major Kuznetzova appeared to be underneath him but I thought she was alive. Brigadier Sutherland was behind the car. He had his pistol in his hand and appeared to have just fired it, so I guessed he would have hit at least one of the enemy. He did not seem to be hurt.

One man was standing with his hands in the air, which I took to be in surrender. There was a briefcase lying on the ground near him. Then I saw Major Kuznetzova get up from under the body of Major Mandelstam. She walked over to the briefcase and picked it up. She opened it and it obviously
contained what we had come to get. I regret to report she then raised her pistol to the man's head and fired. He was killed instantly.

I counted three enemy dead, and on our side one dead, our driver, plus one dead or wounded. Brig. Sutherland attended to Major Mandelstam and reported he was wounded, apparently seriously, but still alive. He and Major Kuznetzova attended to him whilst I checked there was no possibility of anyone else from the other car still being alive.

Of the three enemy dead, I killed one, Brig. Driver had killed Brig. Stewart and Major Kuznetzova had shot Baseyev.

I was concerned about the life of Major Mandelstam but within a few more minutes the Chechen police car returned. There was a lot of shouting but the action was by now over. What happened next was very fast but this is my recollection of it. Within about five minutes of the arrival of the police two more vehicles arrived, army ones. A number of troops got out and there was a brief discussion between the police lieutenant and an army officer, after which the police got back in their car and drove off. The Chechen officer looked down at Major Mandelstam and shouted an order to his men, who put him in the officer's jeep and they drove off. Major Kuznetzova and I were put into the other vehicle and that too was driven off. It was only as we moved off that I realised Brig. Sutherland was not with us. Then I heard a short burst of automatic gunfire. Our driver did not look round. I asked him to stop, as well as Major Kuznetzova, to pick up Brig. Sutherland but he seemed not to hear.

We were driven to the police station, where we found out that Major Mandelstam had been taken to a hospital. We learned later that he was alive. I asked many times about Brig. Sutherland. At first I was told they had been unable to find him, that no-one knew where he was, but then they said they had found his body. I was surprised, as I had seen him alive after the action. I asked about the gunfire we heard as we were driven away but no-one seemed to know anything about that. Major Kuznetzova agreed with me that she had also heard it.

I believe what happened to Brig. Sutherland will never be known. The people concerned are unknown to me and the Chechen authorities have consistently refused to give clear answers to requests for information from my office. Under the circumstances I can only accept the matter is now closed.

I would like also to commend the action of Major Mandelstam to his own government. It is clear that he saved the life of Major Kuznetzova, at very great danger to his own, when he threw himself across her in the line of fire. I would also ask that the sacrifice of Private Gurievitch, our driver, be officially recognised. His extremely prompt action led to the great success of the operation, although he paid the highest price himself.

I must report that I consider the action of Major Kuznetzova was unnecessary. Basyr Baseyev had surrendered and we had the equipment we had set out to get. Nevertheless, we were all under a lot of stress and I admit I may also have done the same thing myself. I leave it to her own commanders to decide what action, if any, to take.

G Drixelius, 12th July 1993

[Editor's note. I believe no action was taken against Marfa.]

JOINT OPERATION IN CHECHNYA, MAY 1993
Lt. Col. Avrom Mandelstam, Golani Brigade*

..... I heard Brigadier Sutherland shout something and realised quickly he had recognised the occupants of the other car. Our driver seemed to understand as well, although as far as we knew he spoke no English. I saw him deliberately pull the steering wheel hard and crash into the other car.

Our car came to a halt just before the embankment by the side of the road. I managed to get the door open and Major Kuznetzova and I got out. We ran for the cover of some bushes where we were able to get out our weapons and prepare to fire them, but no targets presented themselves. I heard a single shot but could not tell where it came from or who had been hit. We did not dare call out and let the enemy know where we were. I left Major Kuznetzova where she was and crept out into the open. As soon as I did I saw a man to one side of me. He saw Major Kuznetzova and raised his weapon. I have no further memory, until some time later when I woke up in the hospital.

A. Mandelstam, 28th June 1993

* Avrom was promoted to Lieutenant-Colonel shortly after his return to Israel. His attachment to the Golani Brigade was, I believe, purely for convenience for the purpose of this report.

REPORT OF MAJOR KUZNETZOVA

..... Our car crashed into the one coming the other way. I did not know why, whether it was an accident. Major Mandelstam seemed to know it was deliberate, that perhaps the other car had hit us for some reason. When we stopped he pushed me out of the door and we managed to get to some bushes nearby. I heard some shouting in different languages. I thought I heard English. When we were hiding in the bushes we both cocked our weapons ready for action. Major Mandelstam then told me to stay where I was and he crawled out. As soon as he did that I saw a man standing the other side of the bushes aiming a gun at me. What happened then was very fast, but I suddenly felt a great weight on me at the same time as hearing the shot. I believe there were other shots, but very quickly. I felt blood on my skin and realised Major Mandelstam had been hit. When I managed to get up, all three enemy were dead, including the man who shot Major Mandelstam. I believe Brig. Sutherland shot Baseyev and the English officer, in which case he certainly saved the life of Major Mandelstam. I would like to place on record his quick thinking and decisive action in the operation.

I recovered the briefcase from the ground and it contained the equipment we had come to obtain.

Brig. Sutherland and I went to help Major Mandelstam. Lt. Gen. Drixelius, the officer from Lithuania, secured the area. The Chechen police returned first, and then some soldiers arrived and the police left. It was very confusing and we were worried about who was in command. Major Mandelstam was quickly put into a vehicle with their officer and taken away. I was put in another vehicle with Lt. Gen. Drixelius, but not Brig. Sutherland. I assumed at that point that he was with Major Mandelstam. As we drive away I heard automatic gunfire, but at that time it did not occur to me Brig, Sutherland might be involved. Lt. Gen. Drixelius asked our driver to stop but he refused. I assumed we would meet up with Brig. Sutherland when we got back, but this did not happen. We were informed later that he was missing.

They told us also that Major Mandelstam was alive and I asked if they would take me to the hospital to see him, which they did. I learned then that Major Mandelstam had saved my life. It was his action in that moment that saved me. He took the shot in the chest and this meant he lost a lot of blood, but the bullet went straight through him at an angle and missed his heart. I would like to record my gratitude to him and to the Israel Defence Forces which he represents.

Major Marfa Kuznetzova
29th June 1993

It was Drixelius who brought the briefcase back. He handed it personally to the British Ambassador in Vilnius, whom he knew and trusted. The Ambassador flew with it to London and handed it to the Foreign Secretary who gave it to the Secretary of State for Defence.

Two weeks later a Russian transport plane landed by special permission at RAF Brize Norton and unloaded two coffins. All of this was secret. At least it was supposed to be secret, but in my experience governments find it just about impossible these days to keep secrets and this was no exception. The following day, a photograph appeared in the Daily Mail of the coffins being unloaded, with a brief story:

The body of Brigadier Alexander Stewart is unloaded at RAF Brize Norton in Oxfordshire. The official word is that Brig. Stewart was killed in an accident but why the secrecy? And who is in the other coffin? Brig. Stewart had recently been transferred to Saudi Arabia, so why is he seen here arriving on a Russian military plane? The Ministry of Defence refused to comment.

The MoD could refuse all they liked but the story suddenly became bigger. The next day the Guardian showed the picture and by ten o'clock even the BBC was showing it on the television news. It was just one picture, and if the MoD had been more clever they could have put this story to bed, but they obfuscated and the media smelled a rat. Before long the papers were showing pictures of Brig. Stewart in Riyadh and asking questions about his relationship with the Saudi Government, and major arms deals with Britain. They wanted to know if there really had been an accident. They showed library pictures of an Ilyushin of the same kind and questions started to be asked about Russian military sales in the region and before long just about everybody had got hold of the wrong end of the stick.

This was an ideal opportunity to let the media get carried away with the wrong story with the inevitable conclusion that would have had but then the politicians started putting their twopenn'orth in. The Defence Secretary started issuing strenuous denials of the story that actually would have deflected the media from the truth, the Opposition called for his resignation without having a clue what he had done wrong and the Prime Minister declared his undying support for a man who had behaved in an exemplary fashion, which worried the Defence Secretary because that was what he usually did before he sacked you.

The papers that were currently supporting the Opposition bayed for blood, so the Prime Minister did what he always did in these situations - he announced an Official Enquiry. It would be worth the millions it would cost to be shot of the problem. The media have to have a story that's still breathing; by the time the Enquiry came to the conclusion that nothing had happened, no-one would be able to remember why it was important in the first place, at least the people who really mattered, the voters.

And that would have been that, except that the story travelled, to America. It wasn't much of a story for the American public but it was enough to arouse CIA interest. A computer somewhere remembered that Brig. Stewart's successor in Moscow was Brig. Montgomery Sutherland, and that was suddenly more interesting. Another computer, in another department of the Secret Service, traced Monty to KTX Industries and then alarm bells started ringing so loudly they could be heard in the White House.

As fast as the British authorities tried to bury it, the Americans started asking awkward questions. The Ambassador in Washington was asked, informally, for information and he did what he was paid to do - say he didn't know anything but would look into it. And that should itself have been enough for a while but there must have been other issues going on that I don't know about because pretty soon the Ambassador was asked back to the State Department to answer questions more formally. He contacted the F.O. immediately and asked for urgent assistance. He was telling the truth when he said he knew nothing, and that was how he would have preferred it, but it wasn't to be. He knew this one wasn't going away.

The British panicked and made a statement about who was in the other coffin - Brigadier Montgomery Sutherland, the recently-appointed military attaché at the British Embassy in Moscow. Digging themselves an ever deeper hole, the F.O. put out a story about some relationship between the two attaches, going back many years to when they had served together in Africa. This was so blatantly untrue it simply brought them closer to the time when someone would have to be sacked. The public have short memories but as soon as Monty Sutherland's name came into the story the papers started dredging up his exploits. Soon, it was headlines like National Hero or National Shame? in the tabloids and not to be outdone The Guardian did a piece asking questions to which there were no answers but which the editor hoped would go down well with his readership. So The Times did an in-depth biography, with testimonials from not only senior officers in the Army but from the Secretary-General of The United Nations himself. That clinched it. Monty was the good guy.

By now though the story had gone truly international, and it wasn't long before it appeared in the Jerusalem Post. Once that happened, it was inevitable that Deborah would find out.

Moscow
17th May 1993

My Dearest Deborah

That you are reading this letter can only be because I am dead. I did not squander my life or give it up without a fight. I believe that fight to be worthwhile, otherwise, I promise you, I would not have risked our happiness for it.

I cannot know how much of what I am about to do will become public, so what I can say on that matter is very limited. But I am afraid it has to be done. We are facing one of the greatest threats to the peace of the world in my lifetime. I have been chosen, by one of the highest authorities, to command this operation, and Avrom, bless him, is by my side. I will do all I can to protect him and with God's blessing he will come through. Meeting him has been one of the best things I have done; your country, and you, can be very proud of him.

Deborah, I don't know now what to say. I thought we were finally to be together but it was not to be. You must know that I have wanted that for a very long time. I fell in love with you in Africa and I have never stopped loving you since, not through my two marriages, or through yours. You have been like a lighthouse through the darkness of the years, showing me the way home.

Writing this, I feel almost like turning back, to safety and a future, but the soldier in me knows I will not do that, will not flinch from my duty.

over to England for her father's funeral. God alone knows what they imagined she had to do with anything, but they have an over-fertile imagination I think, plus a large budget, and they tend towards the belt and braces approach. Especially in the post-cold war age when Congress might reasonably ask what they actually do with all the billions of dollars the American taxpayer forks out. For much of what follows I owe a debt to an American colleague, an investigative journalist whose name, for reasons I am sure you will appreciate, cannot be printed. Much of what he told me could subsequently be verified from other sources.

It didn't take long to discover that equipment was supplied by KTX to USCOM in Norwalk, and that that company had a US Government licence for exports to Moscow. That was enough for the Secretary of State to authorise the CIA to raid KTX Industries. At seven-thirty one morning, just as the early-birds were arriving for work, the Agency descended on KTX's offices like a plague.

First, a ring of police cars surrounded the building and sealed the area off. Then, through this cordon came a convoy of black SUVs which disgorged agents and specialists of every kind. There were computer experts, communications experts, forensic accountants, nuclear security experts (what did they think they were going to find?). There were a lot of people with helmets and automatic weapons, as if they were going into a war zone. All of this was captured on camera by a local radio station's traffic helicopter, before it was ordered to land by the police, by which time it was too late because the pictures were sold by a standing arrangement between the radio station and a television company and broadcast live on the morning news.

Within an hour, the police cordon was itself surrounded by another ring - this time of reporters from every newspaper, radio and TV station that could get a team there. And this being Washington DC, that was a lot. Back in London, the Foreign Secretary watched it on the midday news and could only despair at the American way of doing things. Now, he knew, the cat was well and truly out of the bag. Now, our American allies were going to ask, quite rightly, how much we knew and didn't tell them, information that concerned the security of the Middle East, with the concomitant issues of oil and arms sales that were inextricably linked with it.

It took less than an hour for the searchers to locate the high-security wing as the most likely source of goodies, followed closely by Victor Kurtanjek's office. He hadn't arrived for work that day, having got held up on a flight from Warsaw. Agents were waiting for him at Dulles Airport as his plane landed, and they took him directly to KTX to help them with their enquiries.

They spent the entire day taking the place apart, questioning employees, searching the computers, but they couldn't find anything. It was starting to look embarrassing and senior officers were beginning to look for an exit strategy, scapegoats, that kind of thing, but at half-past six they found it. More precisely, a junior analyst found it. It wasn't something you would even have expected them to be looking for. It was in a file of software instructions, and it was in Arabic. KTX Industries showed no records of having Arab customers.

It took another twenty-four hours for the instructions to be translated into English, and then to be analysed for content. There was no doubt, the only software it could be for was detonation systems for a nuclear device. In fact it matched, almost exactly, the systems KTX had supplied to the US Department of Defense.

CIA stations on every Arab country were put on alert to try to track down the customer. In this, I happen to know from my own sources, they were assisted by the Israeli security services. Iran was out of the frame, being Farsi-speaking, which narrowed it down to Libya, Iraq, Iran and Syria as the most likely candidates, at least initially. Agents in all four countries drew a blank, not necessarily because all four countries were innocent but more because the Americans had a severe shortage of Arabic-speaking agents. In this regard, they were largely dependant on the Israelis.

The breakthrough came from an unexpected source (don't they always?). The Israelis had captured a Hizbollah agent in southern Lebanon and, as he declined to answer their questions, they applied some more vigorous interrogation techniques. They weren't looking for anything in particular, just trawling.

The agent gave them various fairly minor bits of information, some of which they expected to be true, some misinformation. He was, apparently, a cool customer. Except that he had something in his hands that he turned and twisted between his fingers constantly while being questioned. For some reason his interrogators simply ignored it, until it fell out of his hands and one of them picked it up after he had been returned to his cell. It was a piece of plastic strapping, the kind that's used for packaging products up for shipping. And it had stamped on it the shipping company's name and address, in Norwalk, Connecticut.

How this man in Lebanon came to have the strapping is anyone's guess. It was probably one of those unimportant things - perhaps he picked it up from some bin for something to have in his hands, like some people do. To the people who had removed it from the package it protected it was quite meaningless. The man who had it didn't even know the Roman alphabet, so it meant nothing to him at all. It meant something to the IDF Intelligence officer though. Not a lot, but being a very keen second lieutenant he included it in the plastic bag of the prisoner's belongings he forwarded to his headquarters.

They would have disregarded it but perhaps the person who picked it up thought it must be important to have been included and so it got passed up the line again. I don't know any of this, of course. But I can imagine how the chain of events might have taken place, almost with a momentum of their own, until the insignificant strap arrived on the desk of someone who knew they were looking for information about American equipment being supplied to an Arab country. Even he probably didn't make the connection - he just did his job and so did someone else and eventually the innocuous piece of plastic with the incriminating writing on found its way to the Mossad and then the CIA and now they knew that equipment supplied by USCOM had reached Lebanon.

An urgent request went out for the prisoner to be held long enough until a CIA agent could question him. He didn't try to hide anything because he could not conceive of a piece of plastic being a secret. He had picked it up somewhere, he couldn't remember exactly, but it was at a Syrian army base. The Syrians maintained an army of occupation in most of Lebanon, and gave financial and logistical support to Hizbollah. It was almost certain that the circuit board had found its way to Syria via Lebanon. It wasn't absolutely certain, but it was enough.

The CIA went back into KTX Industries as well as USCOM's premises, and tore them apart. Then they went to Victor Kurtanjek's house and tore that apart, upon which his lawyer complained vociferously, so they went to his house and tore that apart as well. In his safe they found the details of a Bahamian bank account in the name of Victor Kurtanjek that contained several million dollars. That traced back to a bank in Chechnya, and that was enough to hang his client.

Then they found documents which made it plain that the

circuit board Monty and his team had brought back from Chechnya was not the first delivered by KTX Industries. There were more weapons.

Within twenty-four hours the President of the United States had been informed. He, in turn, called the Prime Minister of Israel.

Two days later the US Ambassador in Damascus was granted an interview with the Syrian Foreign Minister. He had precise instructions, received by telephone on a secure line from Washington, as to what he was to say. The United States, he said, had credible evidence that the government of Syria had obtained components by false means from an American company with which to assemble a nuclear weapon. The government of the United Sates of America demanded the return of those components, namely printed circuit boards and associated software for use in detonation. The precise wording of the demand is recorded in the State Department's archives, and under the Freedom of Information Act, being non-classified information, is in the public domain.

The Syrian Foreign Minister responded politely and promised to investigate the matter. Three days later the Ambassador was invited to return to the Foreign Ministry, where the Minister informed him, again politely, that his government knew of no such matter and was therefore unable to help the US Government.

The Ambassador duly reported back to Washington and this left the President with a hard decision. He knew, and the Syrians knew he knew, but if he accused them publicly he would have to stand by the accusation, if necessary with force. The American public was in no mood to go charging into Syria after the Gulf war. Would the Syrians call his bluff?

At the cabinet meeting there were the usual hawks and doves. The Defense Secretary was in bullish mood after the liberation of Kuwait and the defeat of Iraq. The Secretary of State wanted time for diplomacy. Everyone else was somewhere in between, which left the President with, if you like, the deciding vote. He went to his ranch to think about it.

Meanwhile, the Israeli Government had no such difficulties. The armed forces were immediately put on a war footing. Israeli diplomats arranged urgent meetings in Cairo and Amman to secure promises that Egypt and Jordan would stay out of any fight. Those countries didn't need long to consider their respective positions and gave the required guarantees. This enabled the combined Israeli tank brigades to mass on the Golan Heights facing Syria. Lorries rumbled through the night from the Dimona nuclear research establishment to Air Force bases in the Negev Desert. All army leave was cancelled, the reserves were called up, the Navy patrolled the Mediterranean to secure the coast. The civilian hospitals were put on war alert and the civilian population were issued with gas masks.

All of this activity was on the television news throughout the world. The US President had to make a decision. As a first step he ordered the US Sixth Fleet to its prearranged battle stations in the Arabian Gulf. US troops in Kuwait and Saudi Arabia were put on a war footing. The US Ambassador in Damascus had another interview with the Foreign Minister, at which he made his government's position clear. Syria must give up any equipment designed for nuclear weapons it had received from US companies, or indeed any other country, immediately.

Or what? The Syrians, it seemed almost inevitably, strung the Americans along. While the world waited with its breath held, with the Middle East on the brink, Syria went about its business as normal. Then Israel made the first move. The Prime Minister called the US President and issued him not with an ultimatum (which would have been presumptuous) but with a statement of fact. If Syria did not comply with America's demand, the IAF would mount a pre-emptive air strike at known Syrian military and research targets.

The US President called the Syrian President and told him this, in a sort of my hands are tied, help me out here way. The Syrian President said no. The US President then called the Israeli Prime Minister and asked him to back down, and he also said no. He said something to the effect that his hands were also tied. The Israeli public had every expectation that in the face of a known threat of this magnitude their government would take any and all actions deemed necessary to protect the country. That included a pre-emptive strike, no matter what the consequences. The Israeli people, and their armed forces, stood squarely behind their government. Could the American President say the same about his country? He didn't know.

The following day, when the President woke up on his ranch, the sun was shining through the windows and as he sat down to his breakfast the world seemed a very normal place. Except that it wasn't. You can only hide for so long. Before he had finished his hash browns the Secretary of State was by his side. Israeli planes were preparing to take off. They had politely informed the US, even giving the targets they had selected. Syrian forces were being rushed to the southern border with Israel and in Lebanon. The President asked the Secretary of State whether the Syrians could take on Israel and the answer was an unequivocal no. They would last no more than a day or two. The Israelis had two choices. They could bomb every conceivable target in the hope of hitting the one that housed the weapon, or they could go in and find it the hard way. Either way, the effect on the Middle East would be catastrophic.

The President scanned that morning's newspapers in an attempt to see which way the wind was blowing. There was the predictable split between the right wing and the left wing. The latter asked what right Israel had to decide which other Middle East nation, other than itself, should be allowed to have nuclear weapons. The President thought this was a fair question and asked his Secretary of State what the answer was. The answer, apparently, was that since Israel had a population of six million and had never made an unprovoked attack on any of its neighbours, and was surrounded by twenty one Arab states with a combined population of 365 million, almost all of whom had at one time or another promised to wipe it off the face of the Earth, the international consensus was likely to be in its favour.

The Secretary of State also ventured the opinion that the US could not now back down and since Israel was going in anyway an awful lot of Americans were waiting for their President to stand and be counted. Add together the Jews, the fundamentalist Christians and a ragbag of people who thought America should shoot first and ask questions later, that was one hell of a lot of voters.

An hour later the President was on the phone to his counterpart in Damascus. He warned the Syrian President that the Israeli Airforce was preparing to take off and that his best advice was to give up the damned weapons or face destruction. The Syrian said there were no such weapons so there was nothing he could do. They stayed on the line, both parties trying to hide their fear. The Secretary of State whispered into the President's ear that the Israeli jets had taken off. They were being monitored by US spy satellites but they didn't need to be. The Israelis were informing their American friends of their every move. They knew they were talking to the Syrians.

The President told the Syrian President the latest development and the Syrian said there was nothing he could do since there were no weapons. As the Israeli F16s crossed into Syrian airspace the phone went quiet. The Syrians had picked them up on their own radar. Very soon they would peel off for their different targets. There was silence on the line, then the Syrian president spoke. He said if the Israelis did not turn back the Syrian Airforce would deliver the three nuclear weapons they had prepared and provoke all-out war. The US President heard the threat and did the greatest thing he had ever done in his political career. He said nothing. He continued to say nothing while the Syrian President sweated. The clock ticked audibly in both Presidents' ears, and they could both see in their minds' eye the Israeli planes in their formations in the Syrian sky. The President of Syria thought he could actually hear them. The silence went on, and the clock ticked.

Then the Syrian broke. He shouted a long string of abuse at the American, mostly in Arabic, and the war was over. Ten minutes later, the F16s banked and turned back for Israeli airspace.

Ministry of Defence
Whitehall
London, SW1

17th August 1993

Dear Dr Kapuchinski

I have been asked by the Secretary of State for Defence to write to you concerning the late Brigadier Montgomery Sutherland. I believe you and Brig. Sutherland were old friends.

The British Government would like you to know that we owe a debt of gratitude to Brigadier Sutherland, as does the world. It has been decided to award him the Military Medal, posthumously, in this country and I know that the government of Israel is considering a similar award, a rare honour for a foreign soldier. The United Nations will also be making a gesture.

A large quantity of letters were found among Brig. Sutherland's effects and I am sure you will want to know that these have been handed over to his daughter, Rosie.

Should there be anything I can do for you, please do not hesitate to contact me.

Yours sincerely
General Thomas Henson
Chief of Manpower, Army Division

Billings, Davenport & Luscombe, Solicitors
Woking
25th August 1993

Dear Dr Kapuchinski

I write concerning the will of the late Brigadier M. Sutherland, which I must advise you is subject to Probate.

A provision was made by Brig. Sutherland in respect of a charity with which I believe you are connected, the Dr Issy Bar-On Foundation. I understand the function of this charity is to train doctors from African states at your hospital in Jerusalem.

Brig. Sutherland was, whilst on active service with the British Army, working undercover as a Vice-President for an American armaments company. He received a salary from that company for almost a year, the entire amount being paid into a bank account which he refused to use. That sum is subject to Income Tax but the amount that will accrue to your charity I calculate at £104,739.26, and in due course I look forward to sending you a cheque for that amount. Perhaps you would be so kind as to let me know to whom the cheque should be made payable.

In addition, Brig. Sutherland made a particular bequest to you personally. Please find enclosed his Distinguished Service Order. The wording of his will is that you should have his 'gong' in remembrance of him. I should be obliged if, while you are writing, you would confirm receipt of this.

If, meanwhile, I can be of any further assistance, please do let me know.

Yours sincerely

Herbert Luscombe, Partner

It was November. Deborah woke up early. She had been doing that lately. The first thing she saw as she opened her eyes was Monty's medal in its frame on her bedside table. Yael was still asleep; she could hear her gently snoring in the next room. She remembered every detail of that day and told me about it much later.

Winter had come early to Jerusalem and the flat was cold. People think Israel is a hot country, but Jerusalem in winter is like a beautiful woman shivering in a summer dress. Deborah put the electric heater on and huddled in front of it with a cup of coffee and a cigarette. She had stopped smoking for a while, but it hadn't lasted long.

By the time she was ready to leave for the hospital the post had been and Yael had picked it up and put all the letters in her mother's bag, like she always did. Deborah dropped her at school and drove on to the Hadassah Hospital. Her position as Chief of Emergency Medicine had become routine and tedious; she was thinking about leaving, just packing up and going. But she hadn't decided. There was her work at the WHO. Perhaps she should apply for a permanent position, but that would mean moving to Switzerland and taking Yael. No, she probably wouldn't do that.

That morning they were expecting a student doctor from Zambia, one of the increased intake Monty's bequest had made possible. Deborah took a close personal interest in these students and that was one thing she was looking forward to.

In the event it turned out to be a busy day, which was good, and it was only that evening when she was at home going through her bag looking for something that she found the letter.

Ein Gedi
11th November 1993

My Dear Deborah

It is going to seem to you like the most terrible trick, but I am writing this letter, in Israel, and I am very much alive.

You see, my love, my death was faked. It was a necessary precaution because there were too many people who might want me dead, so the Ministry of Defence decided to 'kill' me off to prevent that happening.

I have been granted Israeli citizenship by the government here and I even have a new name - a Hebrew one. I have been learning Hebrew with a private tutor. You see, I plan to make my life here. Apart from Avrom, only Rosie knows about this, and I would have told you sooner but there were still some people out there who might have come looking for me. Those people have now been dealt with.

Deborah - I said I am making my life here, but I must add to that that it has always been my hope you will be part of that life. I am writing, rather than coming to Jerusalem, to give you the chance to decide if you want to be. I am asking you, please to come to me, but it will be your choice. Can you forgive me for my deception?

I'm not doing this very well, so I will leave it at that. If you do write, be sure to put my new name on the envelope.

Yours

Monty

[Editor's note. I have not given Monty's new name here, for obvious reasons.]

Jerusalem
14th November 1993

My Darling Monty

Yes.

Love

Deborah

Postscript

Monty was granted Israeli citizenship and he and Deborah are still together. That would make a happy ending to this story, but I hope the reader will forgive me for giving some more detail. There is much I can't say, because our couple are still, in Monty's words, very much alive, and the permission they gave for telling their story came with a condition that Monty's Hebrew name, and their location, would remain a secret. It is also the reason why I have throughout this story sometimes had to be a little sparing with the truth, for which I apologise.

I didn't meet them until long after I had started my research. As I said at the beginning of my story, I had originally been commissioned to write Monty's biography, and the people whose biographies I have written have all been dead. It is, I must say, the first time a subject has come back to life. It is also, I will add, an enormous pleasure that he did. I hope he will not be embarrassed when he reads this (he told me he won't but I doubt him on that) if I say it has been an honour.

And Deborah? I hope it will save her some embarrassment if I simply say that for Monty she was worth the wait. She did leave the hospital but she continued to work occasionally for the WHO and she is still a trustee of the fund set up in Issy's name to train African doctors.

And what of the others whose lives were part of the story?

Avrom Mandelstam, as I said, was promoted to Lieutenant-Colonel. He recovered reasonably well from his wounds, which had been quite serious, but he was never again fit for active duty. The IDF gave him a gong, Etour Hagevora, the highest award for bravery for an Israeli soldier. It was in recognition not only of the operation in

Chechnya but for his years of undercover work. The medal gave his sister immense pleasure.

Major Marfa Kuznetzova emigrated to Israel and married Avrom. She spent two years studying to convert to Judaism (which Avrom didn't ask her to do) and she became an archetypal Jewish wife and mother. They have two boys, one of whom takes after his father in his raffish good looks, the other shy like his mother. I admit to tackling her on the execution of Basyr Baseyev in Chechnya. My feeling is that it was for love of Avrom, whom at that moment she believed Baseyev had killed. I even have a sneaking admiration for a woman who could do that.

Avrom didn't stay in the IDF for long in a desk job. He was a national hero and the Likud Party soon asked him to stand for parliament, the Knesset. He wasn't much of a political animal but I think he was flattered. With a long record of public service, perhaps he saw it as another way of serving his country. If he did, he got a rude awakening. Parliamentary politics in Britain is pretty scruffy but in Israel you have to have a very thick skin indeed. He saw out his term but did not stand at the following general election. He would have been at a loss for what to do next and was thinking of following in Monty's footsteps and becoming what in this country we would call a gentleman farmer. But as soon as he announced his intention not to stand again the Prime Minister offered him the post of Ambassador to the UK. In Israel, unlike here, not all Ambassadors are career diplomats and some posts are handed out as political rewards. Well, the offer was a reward, but Avrom turned out to be an excellent ambassador for his country. I think it fair to say that relations between Britain and Israel, always difficult, have much improved since his arrival in London.

Avrom and Monty have remained firm friends ever since, and, particularly since the death of their father, he and Deborah have been especially close. It seems clear to me that Monty saved Avrom's life in Chechnya, when he shot Alex Stewart, and if Avrom has shown his gratitude with his friendship,

Deborah has never forgotten either. Avrom never fully recovered from the wounds he sustained in Chechnya and sometimes suffers with lung problems. Marfa fusses over him when he isn't well, which I suspect he rather likes.

Yael was fourteen at the time Monty arrived in Israel. She had no idea of his background so her mother simply introduced Monty as a new immigrant from Britain whom she had fallen in love with. Yael lived with them until she went off to the Army and then to university. She followed her father into journalism, not in the Press but on television, and has appeared as a junior news presenter on Israel 1 TV. I think she will do well in her chosen career.

Monty's father died in 1998.

Rosie completed her psychology degree at Gallaudet University in Washington. She has gone on to write and teach, after completing a PhD. Her long-standing partner is also a teacher, a French-Canadian, and the couple live in Montreal. Rosie has learned French, which is an extraordinary accomplishment for a deaf person; she seems to be able to take anything on in life and I don't think it even occurs to her she has a disability. As Monty's situation became less of a security problem, he was finally able to meet Rosie's partner and he tells me his pride in his daughter's achievements knows no bounds. To my surprise it seems Rosie and Yael, the two daughters, have become friends, and they communicate by e-mail regularly.

Rosie's mother, Chloe, developed a drink problem and I'm afraid came to a bad end.

Victor Kurtanjek was charged with a number of offences, some of which verged on treason, but in the end he was given a twenty-year prison sentence and at the time of writing is serving that sentence in the Johnston Correctional Center in North Carolina. Shares in KTX Industries crashed once the news got out about their activities but, because of the important work the company had been doing for the US Defense Department, the US Government allowed much of the company to be bought by one of America's biggest defence contractors, and in due course the shares were worth more than ever. Monty's holding, with all the dividends which he has never touched over the years, will on his death be split equally between Rosie and Yael, so they will both be independently wealthy, and Issy's foundation and Gallaudet University.

Which just leaves Mr Wilson.

Over the years, Monty referred in his memoirs to this name. It was something he worried about from time to time, so did he ever discover Mr Wilson's identity? Yes.

It will be remembered that throughout his career Monty was helped by his father-in-law, Brigadier Rainsford, Chloe's father. He was there to help him after the Jordan debacle, he was responsible for his appointment to Sandhurst, he got him the posting to the United Nations and he sent him Alex Stewart's personnel file, rather too quickly as it happens. So how did a retired officer do all those things?

Because Brig. Rainsford was Mr Wilson. He admitted as much to Monty before he died. The explanation is a strange one. When Monty got into trouble over the Jordan posting, first with the Israeli stamp in his passport and then after he met Deborah in Cyprus and got recalled, the Ministry of Defence put him on a list of officers to be watched. It was a time when certain personnel in the armed forces were suspected of having Communist sympathies. You have to bear in mind that all western governments were worried about the spread of Communism in their infrastructure. Mr Wilson was in fact not one man but a department, a small one of necessity to ensure secrecy. Brig. Rainsford headed that department.

Monty was just one of the officers who came under scrutiny. It wasn't that he was suspected of having Communist sympathies, but simply because Mr Wilson's remit grew to encompass anyone whose loyalty might be in doubt. In fact it seems quite certain now that Brig. Rainsford never thought Monty was a danger. It's true he manipulated his career to ensure he was where the top brass wanted him at any one time, but even Monty had to admit when this came out that these moves had somehow always been to his advantage. I like to think that his father-in-law, faced with the unpalatable task of suspecting his own daughter's husband, decided from the beginning to make the most of it. I think there was even an element of guilt on Brig. Rainsford's part about the way Chloe treated Monty - I suspect he preferred his son-in-law to his daughter. Whatever the case, Monty forgave him. Whether he ever told his former father-in-law that he had at one time suspected him of complicity with Alex Stewart, I don't know. I doubt it.

The final mystery is why Yael, Deborah's daughter, approached me in the first place with information about the letters. I discovered later that my researches had come to the attention of the people who concern themselves with Monty Sutherland's continued safety. They of course told Monty himself that someone was writing his biography and they also advised against letting it happen (which could explain why my researches had been so unsuccessful). He, apparently, disagreed. Why? I think Monty had a distaste for secrecy, having worked with it through most of his army career, starting in Northern Ireland. He also didn't quite share his minders' conviction that he was a marked man. That was probably modesty, which would be in keeping with his character. He didn't really believe he was so important that anyone was going to send a hit squad after him. In that he has since proved wrong, sadly. In fact, as I finish this, there is news that a Hizbollah team has been intercepted by the IDF in the part of Israel where he and Deborah live.....

Jonathan S.
London
October 2008

Printed in Great Britain
by Amazon